"What's wrong,

"I've never been kiss
on a gasp.

He smiled. "Then let's do it again and go for two."

"I'm sorry," she said quickly. "Laredo...I'm not the girl for you."

And then she ran into the Lonely Hearts Salon.

Not the girl for him? Of course she wasn't the girl for him. He wasn't looking for a girl. He was passing through town on his way to Something Big.

But he liked Katy, liked her an awful lot. Wouldn't want to hurt her.

Katy was right—she *wasn't* the woman for him. There would never be a woman for him.

He should never have kissed her....

ABOUT THE AUTHOR

Tina Leonard loves to laugh, which is one of the many reasons she loves writing for Harlequin American Romance. In another lifetime, Tina thought she'd be single and an East Coast fashion buyer forever. The unexpected happened when Tina met Tim again after many years—she hadn't seen him since they'd attended school together from first through eighth grade. They married, and now Tina keeps a close eye on her school-age children's friends! Lisa and Dean keep their mother busy with soccer, gymnastics and horseback riding. They are proud of their mom's "kissy books" and eagerly help her any way they can. Tina hopes readers will enjoy the love of family she writes about in her books. Recently a reviewer wrote, "Leonard had a wonderful sense of the ridiculous," which Tina loved so much she wants it for her epitaph. Right now, however, she's focusing on her wonderful life and writing a lot more romance!

Books by Tina Leonard

HARLEQUIN AMERICAN ROMANCE
748—COWBOY COOTCHIE-COO
758—DADDY'S LITTLE DARLINGS
771—THE MOST ELIGIBLE...DADDY
796—A MATCH MADE IN TEXAS
811—COWBOY BE MINE
829—SURPRISE! SURPRISE!
846—SPECIAL ORDER GROOM
873—HIS ARRANGED MARRIAGE
905—QUADRUPLETS ON THE DOORSTEP
977—FRISCO JOE'S FIANCÉE†
981—LAREDO'S SASSY SWEETHEART†

HARLEQUIN INTRIGUE
576—A MAN OF HONOR

†Cowboys by the Dozen

LAREDO'S SASSY SWEETHEART
Tina Leonard

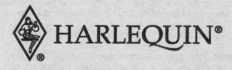

HARLEQUIN®

TORONTO • NEW YORK • LONDON
AMSTERDAM • PARIS • SYDNEY • HAMBURG
STOCKHOLM • ATHENS • TOKYO • MILAN • MADRID
PRAGUE • WARSAW • BUDAPEST • AUCKLAND

ISBN 0-373-16981-7

LAREDO'S SASSY SWEETHEART

Copyright © 2003 by Tina Leonard.

This edition published by arrangement with Harlequin Books S.A.

Visit us at www.eHarlequin.com

Printed in U.S.A.

Many thanks to my readers!
There is never enough I can say
to thank you for your support and your generosity.
This series is for you.
Here also I wish to extend special mention
to the following wonderful people:
LaJoyce Doran, Shadin Quran,
Nicole Christoph, Jeanette Bowman and Beth Reimer.

More than ever, my gratitude goes to the editor angels
at Harlequin who watch over my career—thank you to
Melissa Jeglinski for your many kindnesses
and Stacy Boyd for your calm guidance and patience!

And extra-sloppy, noisy kisses to Lisa and Dean. I adore you
and need the light you bring to my life~~Mumzie.

THE JEFFERSON BROTHERS
OF MALFUNCTION JUNCTION

Mason (37)—He valiantly keeps the ranch and the family together.

Frisco Joe (36)—Newly married, he lives in Texas wine country with his wife and daughter.

Fannin (35)—Should he pack up and head out to find their long-lost father, Maverick?

Laredo (34), twin to Tex—His one passion: to go east and do Something Big with his life.

Tex (34), twin to Laredo—Determined to prove he's settled, he cross-pollinates roses, but can't seem to get them to bloom.

Calhoun (33)—He's been thinking of hitting the rodeo circuit.

Ranger (32), twin to Archer—No one believes him, but he's serious about joining the military.

Archer (32), twin to Ranger—He'll do anything to keep his mind off his brothers' restlessness—even write poetry to his lady pen pal in Australia.

Crockett (30), twin to Navarro—He's an artist who loves to paint portraits—of nudes.

Navarro (30), twin to Crockett—He may join Calhoun in the bull-riding game.

Bandera (26)—He spouts poetry like Whitman—and sometimes nonsense.

Last (25)—Never least, he loves to dispense advice, especially to his brothers.

Chapter One

"A man only fights for the good, boys, not to impose his will on others. Believe in yourself. No one can do that for you. But a real man learns to fight with his brain, not his fists."
—Maverick Jefferson to his sons when they asked him if they could give Sammy Wickle a black eye in kindergarten.

Laredo Jefferson had seen a lot of madness in the past month. The neighbor the twelve Jefferson brothers had known all their lives, Mimi, had become engaged, a startling situation in itself, since the engagement was to someone other than his big brother, Mason. Mason hadn't pulled his head out in time to realize he was going to lose someone who mattered a lot to him—or, at least, Laredo was pretty certain Mimi and Mason meant a lot to each other. Sometimes it was hard to tell if all the preening and poppycock was prideful love or just the wear and tear of a brother-sister relationship.

Frisco Joe had married a fine woman, another surprising development, since, of all twelve brothers, Frisco was the darkest horse, being possessed of an ornerier-than-most nature. Amazingly, Annabelle had certainly sugared him up a bit, and baby Emmie kept Frisco in a constant state of cockeyed grinnyness. It had been a pleasure to watch his sour brother get mowed down by a little mama and her no-bigger-than-a-chickpea baby.

But he was not about to be caught in the same net.

After all the years of drought on their ranch near Union Junction, they'd had a veritable shower of charming female visitors. And it was all he could do to resist paying court to every one of them! Nine new women had come to town from Lonely Hearts Station, a neighboring town. After helping out during last month's terrible storm, the women had decided they would stay.

A lot of bachelors in Union Junction, Texas, had been real happy about that.

Laredo hadn't asked any of the women out on a date. Fidelity was something to be avoided, at least in his opinion. If you were dying of thirst, and someone offered you a huge jug of water, wouldn't you drink as long as you could? he'd reasoned to Mason.

Mason had grunted and told him to go fill the water troughs for the horses. Laredo thought the house was going to be plenty empty without Frisco, and plenty full of Mason and his bad temper. Without Frisco Joe, life wouldn't be the same! Mason had ridden Frisco, Frisco had bucked Mason—without Frisco, Laredo might be next in line to be ridden, and he didn't have Frisco's ability to deal with Mason. Laredo's brothers called him a dreamer, but they usually gave him a pass and picked on his twin, Texas, more, since Tex's passion was growing roses that never bloomed. Budus-interruptus, Frisco had told Tex, that was his problem. Tex had been really steamed, but Laredo had snickered under his sleeve, his face turned from his twin.

Maybe his brothers were getting on his nerves. Maybe they'd lived together too long. Which got him thinking about traveling east—something he'd been thinking about long before the madness of love had hit the ranch. He was in the mood for adventure, a change of pace. Love wasn't going to hit him, he vowed, and picked up his packed duffel bag. He was not about to settle down.

He wanted to do something big.

Without another glance back he left the only home he'd ever known to venture out into the warm March morning. First stop: paying a visit to the Lonely Hearts Beauty Salon, just long enough to say hello to some ladies who'd made his life a little more fun last month. *There* was a place for a troubled man to find a sympathetic ear.

Three hours later he was standing outside the salon, amazed by the hubbub inside—it sounded more like a general meeting place—when suddenly the door flung open. His sleeve firmly grasped in two desperate female hands, he was hauled inside.

He remembered Katy Goodnight, the woman who now had him in her determined grip. He remembered thinking that a man could spend many good nights with a girl like her.

"This is him!" Katy announced to the room at large, which was filled with elderly men, a lot of women and even a pet chicken in a cage on one of the back counters. "This is the man we can enter in the rodeo as the champion for Lonely Hearts Station, Texas. If anyone can ride Bloodthirsty Black, it's Laredo Jefferson. Ladies and gentlemen, pay homage to your champion, and the man who can whup the daylights out of our rival, the Never Lonely Cut-N-Gurls and their bull, Bad-Ass Blue!"

Voices huzzahed, hands clapped, Katy released his shirt so she could clap, too, and even the chicken uttered a startled squawk. But no one was more startled than Laredo to be picked as some kind of bull-riding savior.

He'd never ridden a bull in his life.

Katy whispered, "You got here just in the nick of time. You're my hero!"

He swallowed, and decided to keep his mouth shut. After all, he'd been looking for a little adventure—and it wasn't every day a man got to be a hero to a woman named Goodnight.

KATY KNEW that desperation had just opened the door and sent her a man—a man who looked as if he could solve her problem. Laredo was big enough to hang on to an ornery, few thousand pounds of irritated horns-and-hooves. He was strong, judging by the muscles in his forearms and the biceps not covered by a short-sleeved red T-shirt. That area below the leather belt and covered by nicely fitted blue jeans looked healthy, as well—guaranteed to fit in a saddle and keep a seat well past the eight-second horn.

He was sexy as all get-out, too—a strong chin, square face and simmering dark eyes under a summer-weight western hat set her heart to jumping just like mad Bloodthirsty Black when he shook off lesser handlers. But sex appeal had nothing to do with her mission.

All she needed was a man who could hang on for eight seconds. Was that so much to ask?

Maybe hanging on wasn't what Laredo wanted— by the look on his face, she'd completely startled him with her announcement—but matters being what they were, she'd have to take the chance that his gentlemanly instincts would overcome his shock.

Their last bull rider had backed out after the Never Lonely Cut-N-Gurls sank their claws into him, filling his ears with stories. Katy had a vague idea what stories might be told in the salon across the street. Remembering her ex-fiancé, Stanley, wrapped around her ex-best friend, Becky, in the bridal changing room in the church, she had an inkling they were *bedtime* stories.

She eyed Laredo with eyes that missed nothing, and realized that if the Never Lonely girls had set an all-out campaign for the previous rider the Lonely

Hearts girls had sent into the arena, Laredo had about a sixty-minute shelf life before he was discovered by the enemy.

And lured away.

Temptation must be avoided at all costs.

Because Miss Delilah, the owner of the Lonely Hearts Salon, really, really needed a champion. Katy's boss—and rescuer—Delilah, was looking for something big, something miraculous to happen for her salon. It housed the closest thing to real family Katy had ever known. So unless he turned her down, something big and miraculous was what Laredo Jefferson was going to be, Katy determined, staring up at him as he stared down at her, apparently rooted to the floor in his big boots. If she weren't so desperate, she'd have time to appreciate the scenery, but as it was, time was limited.

Please let him say yes, she prayed, gazing up into those beautiful, stunned eyes.

Or at least don't let him shrug her off like the crazy woman she knew she must seem to be. She'd never had much luck with men—in fact, her ex-fiancé was right now enjoying her ex-best friend's thong in the south of France on a honeymoon *Katy* had planned—but, she wasn't really frigid. She was certain her heart was warmer than an ice cube, no matter what Stanley said. Being a virgin wasn't a crime…naiveté was unfortunate, perhaps, but it wasn't prissy, uncaring virtue she'd been wearing like a steel-plated hymen. It was just…innocence.

Or maybe, she thought suddenly, as she dimly

realized Laredo had gorgeous dark-coffee-colored eyes that were dilated and focused on her with a heat matched only by the sun outside, maybe it was uncertainty that had kept her a virgin.

Uncertainty may have frozen her once, but today was a new day, and Laredo was not Stanley. She took a deep breath and forced her best cajoling tone. "So, what do you say, cowboy?" she asked softly.

"Little lady," he finally said, finding the voice she'd shocked out of him. "We have a problem."

Her throat dried out. A problem. That didn't sound like a yes, did it? She could feel all her sister stylists watching them, could feel their breath held as tightly in their chests as hers was. "Problem?"

His eyes softened as he nodded. "Would you care to talk about it, maybe outside?" he asked.

Slowly she released his sleeve, which she'd been clutching since she'd dragged him inside the salon. "All right, Laredo." She glanced around at everyone in the salon. "I'll be right back."

Not towing a hero, maybe, and minus her paltry self-confidence. Not that her self-confidence was the main thing, of course. If Laredo couldn't be the hero they were looking for, then time was paramount. They'd have to find another hero.

The rodeo was in four days, and someone had to ride their bull. Lord only knew she'd fantasized about riding it herself, to save Delilah from her sister, Marvella, who owned the competing salon across the street. Marvella's salon had just about finished off Miss Delilah's honest way of work.

Because, rumor had it, it wasn't just a close shave being sold across the street by the Never Lonely girls, which left Miss Delilah with very few clients indeed. She'd had to let half her staff go last month. Fortunately, Union Junction had welcomed the nine newcomers. Yet, how cruel of Marvella to deliberately set out to ruin her own sister!

Not yet, Katy told herself, as Laredo closed the salon door behind them. Not if she had anything to do with it.

Outside, the sun shone brightly on the pavement. If it was possible, Laredo looked even more handsome in bright light.

Flirting skills. Enticement. Clearly, she was lacking in some womanly fundamentals, she decided. Because Becky, her ex-best friend, who even now was no doubt having her thong removed by the apparently lusty Stanley Katy had never known, would have roped, tied and thrown Laredo to the ground, all without doing much more than smiling. Rolling her hips. Showing pretty knees beneath her daily miniskirt parade.

Becky would have had a yes out of Laredo before he'd even drawn another breath.

That didn't mean she was sexless or frigid, Katy assured herself. It just meant she hadn't ever tried flirting. She didn't get an F just because she didn't take the course.

She took a deep breath, marshaled up her best Barbie smile, widened her eyes and sucked in her stomach so her breasts would at least marginally appear through her linen ankle-length dress—a move she was copying straight from the Never Lonely Cut-N-Gurl handbook. Her posture thrown off by the sudden stiffness, Katy placed a hand on Laredo's forearm for support, which he gallantly covered with his other hand, as if she truly were a doll worth holding! Maybe Becky had been onto something with all that gooey a-man-is-made-to-be-adored stuff. "You were going to tell me about a teensy little ol' problem, Laredo?" she asked, so sweetly she was certain sugar drizzled out of her mouth. "I'm just positive a man like you never lets a little ol' bump in the road stop him."

He nodded, frowning, seemingly flustered by her full-force display of flirt-go-ditz.

"I've never ridden a bull," Laredo said.

THE EXPRESSION on Katy's face was no longer hero worship, and Laredo felt as if all the air had been let out of him. Bam! Just like that, he was an ordinary mortal again. And here he'd been dreaming of doing something big with his life.

"Never ridden a bull," Katy murmured, as if she couldn't believe her ears. "But you live at the Malfunction Junction Ranch. All your brothers bull ride. I saw the ribbons and trophies. There must have been hundreds."

He shook his head. "Not me, though. Mason figured I was the one most likely to have a wandering foot that'd take to the rodeo lifestyle permanently. It's one of the very few things I would admit that my brother guessed right about me. And Last never has, either, but that's because he was the baby and Mason didn't have time to teach him to ride much of anything except a horse. Actually, Last never really did learn to ride a horse very well.'' He realized he was babbling, trying to fill in space so he wouldn't have to finish letting Katy down.

''Wandering foot?'' Katy repeated. ''What does that have to do with staying on a bull?''

He ran a gentle finger along the curve of her chin. God, how he hated disappointing her. She really was a cute little thing in her sandals and long dress, just like a girl playing dress-up in her mother's clothes. He liked the fact that she had little or no makeup on. Her hair was a bit ruffled, which he wouldn't have expected for someone who worked in a beauty salon. Everything about her seemed somehow fresh and innocent, from her big blue eyes to the dark bangs that framed them. ''Mason was determined to keep our family together. It's a long story, but it has to do with the fact that our father left when most of us were young and Mason got stuck with the details of parenting. He made decisions the best he could. Sometimes he was wrong. But most of the time, he was dead-on.''

''So you're a restless type.''

''That's right.''

She pulled her chin away from his finger. ''I wouldn't know the feeling.''

He eyed her, knowing that she wouldn't find that adjective attractive in a man. But that was okay, because he wasn't trying to suit himself up to be attractive to her. "I don't suspect you would."

"So you never got to ride a bull?"

"I could have sneaked around. Last wasn't supposed to, either, but he did just the same. Mason didn't want the baby of the family busting himself up."

"Of course not," she murmured.

"But Last has always done whatever he pleased."

She glanced up at him. "But you obeyed your brother."

He shrugged. "I couldn't quibble with his logic. I didn't want the family separated myself, and I wouldn't have been the one to do it. No one else seemed to have a hankering to leave the ranch like I did."

"You've left now," she said.

"Yes."

Hope flared in her eyes. "Maybe now is the time to disobey Mason about bull riding!"

He laughed. "I don't have to obey him anymore. But I wouldn't be any good at riding, Katy. I never learned. And there's more to it than getting on."

She looked as if she might cry any second.

"Here," he said gently, "let's take a walk. Tell me what's going on, and maybe I can help you resolve your situation."

"I need a hero," she said stubbornly.

He placed a hand dramatically over his chest. "I promise I think better than I ride. Come on. Walk and talk."

She sighed, not liking his offer one bit, but clearly seeing no way to refuse. "There's a lot at stake."

"You don't look like the kind of girl who hangs around rodeos, Katy." He eyed her curves underneath her long dress with appreciation. She'd look mighty fine in blue jeans—

"I'm not," she said as they began to walk side by side. She glanced up, almost catching him eyeing those curves. "Until last week, I'd never even seen a bull up close."

"What happened last week?" He couldn't resist asking since her head had drooped, her pretty sable-colored hair swinging forward as she spoke. "Tell Uncle Laredo."

She shot him a wry look. "You are not my uncle, cowboy."

"Oh, that's right. I'm supposed to be the hero. Only I got shot off my horse."

"Bull, not horse." She sighed. "Every year Miss Delilah buys a bull from one of the local FFA kids. The kids raise their bulls, usually from the time they were born, until they auction them at the fair. This pays for college and other expenses. Then Delilah enters her bull in certain events, such as riding, and best hoof painting."

"Hoof painting?" He put out a hand to slow her determined gait. "You act like you're marching on the enemy yourself. What's best hoof painting?"

"It's sort of a paint-your-nails-for-bulls event. Only it's the hooves that get painted as pretty as they can possibly be. Flowers, doodles, Indian sunsets, you name it. On an animal that won't stay still. It's a mental and physical challenge.''

''I've never heard of that.''

''Miss Delilah thought it up.''

''Of course.'' It sounded like a beauty salon owner's idea.

''Don't sound so snickery. Miss Delilah raises a lot of money for charity with her contests. People come from miles around to enter. And then, when the fair comes to town the following year, she sells the bull to the restaurant in Texas that bids the most for it. By then, everybody's seen her bull for that year, in several events, and they bid it pretty high. With this money, she's been able to keep her salon open.'' Katy shook her head sadly. ''Everyone wins, you know. The student who raised the bull, Lonely Hearts Station charities, a lucky restaurant and Miss Delilah's favorite charity, taking in women who need a helping hand. But not since the Never Lonely girls opened up their salon.''

She tossed her head in the direction of a business no one could miss—almost the red-light establishment of beauty salons with a neon sign sure to light up a dark sky and all manner of lip prints painted on the windows. ''Rivals, huh?''

''Delilah's sister, Marvella, runs that shop, and she wants nothing more than to put Delilah out of business. And her weapon of the moment is a bull named Bad-Ass Blue.''

Laredo would have laughed, except, by the serious stiffness in Katy's back, he knew he'd better swallow the laughter fast. "So, how does a bull ruin Miss Delilah's shop?"

"By getting more attention. By having a rider that knows how to showboat. By luring our rider into missing his ride," Katy said bitterly. "Bloodthirsty Black never even got out of the chute because we didn't have a rider."

Laredo was afraid to ask, but he had to know. "And the best-hoof-painting contest? How did Bloodthirsty Black fare in that?"

"Not at all," Katy said. "Someone slipped a baby mouse into his stall and he darn near broke it down trying to crush the poor thing. After that no one dared get near him."

Laredo shook his head. "No one plants a mouse. They just hang around livestock areas."

"Not this one. It still had the price tag on it."

He couldn't help a chuckle now, which earned him a rebuking stare from Katy. "They don't put price tags on mice, Katy."

"This one was wearing a red price tag on his back. Two dollars and ninety-eight cents," she said definitively.

Laredo was positive she was giving him a tall tale. "A marked-down mouse, I guess."

She instantly halted, putting her fists on her hips. It was a gesture he kind of thought looked good on her, even though any sane man shied away from a ticked-off female. "There is nothing funny about Miss Delilah's dilemma. If you were truly my hero, you would know that this is a serious matter."

That stung, far worse than it should have. So much for doing something big—he couldn't even pass a small hero's test like not laughing at a story aimed to make him look like a patsy. "I'm sorry," he said earnestly.

"You certainly should be. It's not gentlemanly to laugh at people's livelihoods."

He hadn't thought of it that way, and Katy was right. In silence they began to walk again, more companionably now since he'd proffered an apology. "Okay, say the price tag on the mouse was a coincidence. Maybe it had run through a bag and picked it up accidentally."

"Maybe, but I don't think so. It was from a store in Dallas."

"But it could have been something someone brought to the rodeo," he insisted. "What's the purpose of leaving a price tag on a mouse? It basically alerts you to the fact that there's been cheating and sabotage."

"But that's the intimidation factor. They have never cared that we know what they're doing. Who's to stop them? All the younger men in this town go to that salon, including the sheriff. We get the wives, who want no part of what goes on over there."

"And that's another thing. Have you ever been inside the salon? Tried their services?"

"No."

"So how do you know that this is all deliberate?"

"They lured our cowboy into their salon, they got

him drunk—and possibly more—on the day he was supposed to ride. What assumption would you draw from that?''

"That he was a lazy cowboy, and maybe not even a real bull rider, Katy. Did you ever think of that?"

"He had a buckle and all kinds of pictures of him with other trophies.''

Laredo sighed, knowing any of that could have been bought or finagled. Katy, as earnest as she was, seemed the type people might take advantage of. She was so sweet and trusting and open. A marked-down mouse, indeed. Why would a rival salon go to the trouble of bringing in a mouse with a red tag when they could have spooked the bull any number of ways? "So, if the rodeo is already over, why do you need another rider?"

"Because Miss Delilah raised a huge stink and called Marvella and told her that she knew she'd cheated and that if there wasn't a rematch, she was going to burn the Never Lonely Cut-N-Gurls Salon to the ground.''

"She did that?" This didn't sound like the woman who had come out to Malfunction Junction with twenty women and one baby, who had taken care of eleven cowboys and a truck driver during one of winter's worst storms. That woman had seemed very sane and practical. "I'm having trouble with Miss Delilah being a lawbreaker and an arsonist.''

"We'll never know, because her sister agreed to a rematch. The thing is, though, I think it's a setup,''

Katy whispered, stopping to gaze up into his eyes. Laredo felt his heart go thud and then boom as he tried to inhale. Then exhale. Katy's eyes widened, drawing him in. "I think a red-lined mouse was child's play to Marvella. Call me gullible if you will, and trusting, but I was recently duped by a girl who was just like a sister to me."

"You don't say," Laredo breathed, trying real hard to sound surprised.

She nodded. "So I know what women are capable of."

"I'm sure you do."

"And I know Miss Delilah's getting set up on this."

"What could Marvella do?"

Katy's gaze swept over his shoulders and then across his chest. "I don't know. But she will send her girls to steal my hero."

His mouth dried out at the thought of a bunch of women coming after him with their feminine lures. It wasn't an altogether unhappy vision.

But the words from Katy's mouth had perked up his heart. He could be her hero. He could do it. He was not the kind of guy to make a promise and then cut and run.

"You can count on me," he said.

"You'll ride Bloodthirsty Black?" she asked on a gasp.

"I'll probably get stomped by his brightly painted hooves, but then at least everybody will know about the hard-wired bull Miss Delilah's got for sale. Then the charities will be happy, and a restaurant will be happy, and some FFA kids will be happy—"

"*I'll* be happy." She threw her arms around his neck by launching her small body up against his chest, leaving about twelve inches dangling between her feet and the sidewalk. "Thank you, Laredo. I knew I could count on you!"

He would call Mason tomorrow, he thought, and get some tips on how to stay on a beast from hell. Right now he was just going to stand here and smell Katy Goodnight's perfume, and try not to think about how sweet a girl like her would be in his bed.

And then again, maybe thinking about how sweet she'd be in his bed was exactly why he'd said he'd ride her darn bull. He hadn't been kidding when he said he'd probably get stomped.

"So," he said into her hair as he held her against him, "what happened to the mouse?"

"I rescued her," Katy murmured. "When Bloodthirsty kicked in the stall, she ran out, and I scooped her up before she could run into another stall to get crushed by a different bull."

"Her?"

"There are only girls in our salon. We named her Rose, and she sleeps in a little box beside my bed."

Oh, boy. "Lucky mouse," he muttered.

"What?"

"Nothing," he said quickly. "I just can't wait to ride that bull," he fibbed.

"Think you can stay on eight seconds?"

He squeezed her to him, breathing in deeply.

"I'm positive I have much longer than eight seconds in me."

"Really?"

"Well," he said hastily, switching gears from sexual to realistic, "I don't expect I'll be that good."

She smiled at him luminously. "Since it's your first time and all."

He swallowed, his Adam's apple jerking in his neck like a double knot on a child's tennis shoe. "Yeah."

"Do you have a place to stay for the night, Laredo?"

His throat tightened. Was he about to receive an invitation of the best sort? "No."

"Then you can sleep in my room."

Heaven! Hallelujah! Doing something big in his life was turning out to be so easy. Why hadn't he been adventuresome sooner?

"And I'll sleep with Miss Delilah," she continued.

His enthusiasm withered like day-old soda pop. He set her down on the concrete. "I'd hate to put you out."

"It's the least I can do for the man who's going to single-handedly save our salon."

He nodded jerkily, trying to look appreciative.

"And we're fixing wilted lettuce and greens for dinner."

He pasted a smile on his face, thinking that if the menu was always so green and healthy, he wouldn't have to ride Bloodthirsty Black. He'd just gnaw the steak-on-the-hoof to death and chalk up an easy win that way. "Thank you," he repeated.

"Let's go back and tell everyone what you've decided," Katy said, delighted.

"Oh, yes. By all means," he agreed reluctantly. Longingly he glanced across the street, where a stunning blonde was deliberately trying to catch his gaze through the window. She was wearing a red shirt tied at the waist, and, even at this distance, he could tell she was a very healthy girl. To his surprise, she held a sign to the window that read Free Meal to Travelers in bold red, glittery letters.

Beside him Katy floated along, oblivious to the exchange. To be polite—because he'd only heard one side of the story, after all—he tipped his straw western hat to the blonde and then shook his head in the negative.

Fair was fair, and no matter how bright the invitation across the way—even if they served steak and mashed potatoes—he was going to be a man Katy could trust.

Chapter Two

"So what exactly was the big problem?" Hannah Hotchkiss asked as she walked into Katy's bedroom.

"Problem?" Katy asked, eyeing her best friend and companion stylist warily.

"The one Laredo mentioned. By the time the two of you returned from your walk, you had a yes out of him, and he was wearing a distinctly cattywhumpussed expression."

"A minor detail," Katy murmured. "Nothing that was truly a problem." She wasn't about to share the worrisome detail that their knight in shining armor lacked experience in the saddle.

"I think you've caught that man's eye."

Katy glanced up, horrified. "Do not say that. He is not my type at all."

"What is your type?"

Stanley came to mind, but Katy tossed that thought violently out of her brain. "I haven't figured it out yet. But I'm certain I'll know it when I see it." She blew her bangs away from her forehead.

"These bangs will not grow fast enough to suit me."

"Why are you letting them grow out? They suit your face and showcase your eyes."

"I look like a little girl. I don't want to look like that anymore." She handed a picture to her friend of a model dressed like a ballerina, her hair pulled away from her face in a severe topknot. "That's the way I want to look."

"Like you haven't had a good meal in a month?"

Katy snatched the paper back. "Elegant. Sophisticated."

"Like you don't give a damn."

"Exactly." Katy nodded. "I don't."

"Now you just have to convince yourself."

"Right."

"What a bozo that Stanley must have been." Hannah sighed and got to her feet. "Listen, pulling your hair back until you look like a scarecrow isn't going to give you the mature edge you're looking for."

"You have a suggestion for maturing a permanent baby face?"

"No. The baby face is not the problem—and, by the way, it's called a cute face. There's nothing baby about you. Your challenge is to become more daring. *Daring.* Remember that word."

Katy raised a brow.

"You're masking your real worry by making it a hair issue, something all women do, and sometimes men, as well. The key is to face the issue dead-on, and pin it on the body part where it actually belongs. It's never a hair issue. Could be the brain, could be the breasts, could be your—''

''I don't need a body catalogue,'' Katy interrupted.

''So, where's your real issue?''

''My heart.''

''Not possible. Choosing the heart is a stall tactic. It means you're still transposing and referring your denial. The heart is not part of the equation, as it is only a label for people's emotions. A visual, if you will.''

''I don't know if I will or not.'' Katy groaned, unwilling to go down the path. ''My womanhood,'' she finally said. ''If I'd been more of a woman, even Becky couldn't have gotten Stanley away from me.''

''That's a myth, you know. Women successfully steal men all the time. It doesn't take much effort.''

''I will never believe that. There are a few men out there who have antitheft devices on their hearts.''

''Yes, but we're not talking about their hearts, and I have it on good authority that antitheft devices do not fit on a man's p—''

''All right!'' Katy interrupted. ''So any man is ripe for the picking. Then what's the point of me trying to overcome *my* issue if *their* issue is unsolvable?''

''Because once you develop more confidence, your chance of a man ever straying from you is dramatically diminished. You put a certain amount of color on a lady's hair to diminish her gray, don't you?''

"Yes," Katy said uncertainly.

"Well, you have to wear confidence to attract and keep someone you love. Become a bright, new color. Remember our new word—*daring*.''

"Lack of confidence was not why Stanley married Becky.''

"He did that because he was already at the church, the guests had flown in, his mother was wearing Bob Mackie, and you, my sweet gullible angel, had footed the bill as the bride. Plus, he still had a smile on his face from what had occurred in the bridal changing room. Strategically, if he couldn't wait another five minutes or so to enjoy your virginity, I'm thinking he didn't have much staying power for the long haul. Not that I'm judging him, exactly, since I have never met him. However, sometimes actions speak louder than words, and I sincerely believe your wedding day was one of those loud action moments.'' Hannah examined her nails casually. "By the way, you *are* going to send his parents a bill for the wedding.''

Katy gasped. "Maybe Stanley and Becky, but not his parents!''

"No way. His parents are filthy rich and worried about impressions. You got the shaft and they'll be anxious to make certain you don't pay for their son's cruel indiscretion, lest you tell someone important like…Dear Abby. Oprah, even. The whole matter sounds very Jerry Springer to me. That'll hit Stanley's parents where they panic, and they'll certainly cough up what you're owed.''

Katy flushed, hating the humiliation she'd suffered that day. ''I want to keep it quiet. Forget about it. Move on.''

''You are *not* as confident as you could be, Katy,'' Hannah said softly. ''And under the circumstances, I understand. But by the time I'm finished with you, confidence will radiate from you!''

She wondered what Laredo saw radiating from her. Messy ponytail and no lipstick—probably all he saw was a dull aura. ''Okay, do your darnedest. I guess.''

Hannah lifted Katy's ponytail and ran it through her hand; Katy could practically hear her friend's creative brain whirring away.

Sighing, she reminded herself that she'd come to work at the Lonely Hearts Salon for just this reason. She needed the emotional support of women to help her get over her deepest fear: that she was sexually dysfunctional. Truth was, it hadn't been all that hard to keep her virginity. She had never felt a point-of-no-return reason to surrender it. But her best friend was talking about men as if they were as easy to pick as a dessert from a menu, and for Katy that would never be the case. It would take a kind and gentle man eons to teach her any differently. ''I'm like Rapunzel. Locked in my own ivory tower.''

''I think you should experiment on Laredo Jefferson, Katy. I believe romancing that man could knock a few bricks out of your tower. Rattle the foundation a bit.''

Katy shook her head. ''The last person who could ever save me from myself would be the freewheeling Laredo Jefferson. I've been to his home at the Malfunction Junction Ranch, and his family is wild and woolly. Fun, but too much for a girl like me.'' She shrugged. ''Anyway, someone once told me that an ivory tower is really a phallic symbol—in Laredo's case, I'd believe it! And right now, this is just a stop on his eastward hunt for adventure, so I'd never dream of allowing him to scale my walls. Even if he wanted to.''

''See, there you go again. *If*. Of course he does!''

''Do you really think so?'' Katy asked doubtfully.

''A man does not agree to ride a bull unless he's fairly sure there's a helluva prize waiting for him once he's hit the dirt, honey.''

Katy straightened. ''I don't think of myself in those terms.''

''Wait till I'm done with you. You'll be thinking Scarlet O'Hara by Saturday. I promise.''

''Scarlet O'Hara was a flirt, a maneater,'' Katy protested.

''Exactly.''

''You're doing what?'' Mason shouted in Laredo's ear over the phone. ''Have you clean lost your mind?''

Laredo pictured Katy's concerned face. ''Not lost

it, just temporarily misplaced it, maybe. Mason, I need some tips.''

''You want a phone course in killing yourself by stupidity.''

''Someone has to do this, and it's going to be me.''

''Obviously,'' Mason muttered. ''This is not what I thought you meant when you said you were heading back east for adventure. You've barely left the county!''

''You know what they say about one's own backyard.''

''Oh, hell.'' There was an audible sigh from the other end of the line. ''I guess I'll send Tex over with the gear you're going to need.''

''Tex won't want to be torn away from his roses right now,'' Laredo warned. ''He's right in the middle of preparing for the oncoming spring season.''

''I'll hire Martha Stewart to baby-sit his buds,'' Mason growled. ''In the meantime, Tex can come out there and share his vast knowledge with you.''

Somehow, the idea of his twin coming out and spending time around Katy wasn't altogether appealing. ''Well—''

''I can't give you pointers by phone, if you're determined to do this. What's the name of the bull, by the way?''

''Bloodthirsty Black.''

''Is he a first-night bull or a marquee bull?''

Laredo scratched his head. ''He's an unknown

quantity. The last cowboy who was supposed to ride him had a change of plans.''

''Maybe he was smart.''

Any man who chose having sex over bull riding probably had some sense. Laredo squinted around Katy's room. Her bed was unrumpled and covered with a clean, white cotton bedspread. There were white lace curtains floating at the open window. Beside her bed, Rose the mouse stared up at Laredo, her pink-flesh ears and tiny paws quivering. She was smaller than his little finger, and for a mouse, quite adorable. Her red price tag was stuck on the side of her wire-covered box as a pretend welcome mat. Katy had drawn a door above the welcome mat, and placed paper lace cutouts around fake windows. Laredo sighed to himself, then sat straight up as he realized something white and lacy was poking out from under Katy's pillow.

Gingerly, he tugged the lace. It left its hiding place with a smooth, gliding flash of froth. Holding it up, he realized it was sheer, it was very short, and Katy slept in this at night. His pulse raced as he glanced toward the door. He was pretty certain Katy wouldn't appreciate walking in and finding him with her nightgown in his hands and very little room left in his jeans.

''Laredo?'' Mason's voice asked in his ear. ''Laredo!''

Having sex or riding a bull.

He hadn't been offered sex. But occasionally a lucky hero got gifted with such a prize. Shoving the nightgown back under the pillow, he said, "I'm riding that bull, Mason, come hell or high water."

"DID YOU GIRLS NOTICE the new man in town?" Marvella asked as she stared out at her sister's salon.

"Did we ever!" her girls chorused.

"Looked like a *real* cowboy to me," Marvella said. "I so love cowboys! I do wonder how Delilah keeps coming up with these timely miracles."

"I've got first dibs," a stylish brunette called. "It's my turn for a new customer."

"Honey, he's not a customer till you convince him he is," someone corrected her. "And all's fair in love until the moment one of us closes the bedroom door."

"I wouldn't say it's over just because the door closes," someone said. "If I recall, one of you managed to be in the bed waiting, while you had a fake phone call downstairs for the girl he thought he was going to be spending the night with."

A few giggles went round the room, and a redhead in the corner blushed uncomfortably. "I should have known it was a trick. Extra points for creativity, especially since he didn't seem to mind the switch," she said.

"Well, this cowboy isn't going to get his eight seconds onboard Bloodthirsty Black. If Delilah wants to be humiliated twice, we can accommodate her," Marvella said. "But we can't be obvious, because I can guarantee you, he's been told in detail how truly mean, unkind and positively sex-starved

we are. Delilah will be extracautious this time.'' She
tapped long fingernails against the windowsill. "In
four days. I don't want him to even lay a leg over
Bloodthirsty Black. This calls for sweetness and
light, and dainty coincidence.''

"Dainty?"

"Did you see that he was escorting Katy Goodnight on a walk? That's dainty as powdered sugar
on a doughnut,'' Marvella pointed out.

"If her fiancé ditched her at the altar and married
her best friend, she's got something missing in her
sugar bowl,'' someone suggested. "Dainty is not always delightful.''

"Okay,'' Marvella said with a snap of her fingers.
"I've got just the plan.''

"Is it dainty?"

She smiled as she watched the lights coming on
inside her sister's salon. "No,'' she said. "It's a
doozy.''

Chapter Three

The next morning Laredo met his brothers at the arena so they could get an eyeful of Bloodthirsty Black in his holding pen. The bull looked as if he had only ten more seconds before he busted out another perfectly good stall. Stepping back so they wouldn't irritate the bull more, Tex and Ranger shook their heads in unison.

"You're a nut," Ranger said. "You're going to need spine replacement if you ride him."

Laredo glared at him. "Tex is the one who's coaching me. You just came along for the laugh."

Tex shrugged. "He came along to keep me company on the ride, and mainly to try to help me talk you out of getting yourself killed. How's your health insurance, by the way? Both physical and mental? Maybe you should see a head shrink before you do this, 'cause I think you may have left your brains back in puberty."

Twin or no, Laredo was duty-bound to argue. "If

I was deranged, I wouldn't be calling for reinforcement. Now, shut up and start coaching.''

"Let me ride him for you," Ranger offered. "The Lonely Hearts girls just need a champion. They don't care who it is."

"It's gonna be me," Laredo said stubbornly.

"Why?" Tex demanded. "Ranger has the most wins besides me."

"He's too old. That was ten years ago."

"Excuse me?" Ranger said. "I'm thirty-two. You are thirty-four. How am I too old?"

"Because you've always been old. Me, I'm just now trying to find myself. This is my midlife crisis," Laredo said proudly, staring at Bloodthirsty Black. "All two to three thousand pounds of it."

"Sheesh. Other men want a pretty woman. My twin wants a head-and-neck rearrangement from an animal born to hate him. Makes perfect sense to me."

Ranger chuckled. "If Laredo's suffering a crisis, does that mean you are too, Tex?"

"Just because Archer's spending all his time writing to a Nicole Kidman look-alike in Australia, does that mean you're burning up the stationery with Byronic sonnets?" Tex jutted his chin. "Pull your head out, Ranger. Being twins does not mean we're split halves of the same person, as you very well know!"

Bicker, bitch, battle. For a moment Laredo thought his whole big fantasy of being a hero might go flushing downstream, until Katy Goodnight rounded the corner, bearing a basket with a cherry-printed cloth napkin inside. Instantly his whole day brightened. "Hi, Katy," he said with a big grin he couldn't control.

"Hi, Laredo," she said with a smile, before turning to his brothers. "And another Laredo," she said to Tex. "I'm sorry, I shouldn't have forgotten your name since I met you only a month ago, but I do remember your face," she said to Ranger.

"Well, that's all that's important," he said gallantly. "If a pretty gal just remembers my face—"

"Howdy, fellas," said another female voice.

They all turned as Hannah Hotchkiss came into view, carrying a basket decorated with blueberry sprigs. "This is Hannah," Laredo began, then ceased his introduction when he realized Ranger had nearly swallowed his teeth as she smiled up into his face. "Ranger," Laredo said sternly, "this is Katy's best friend."

"We brought you a snack," Hannah said. "We didn't know you had company, Laredo. But we have plenty."

Ranger took the basket from her and peeked inside. "Mmm. Cookies and strawberries. My favorite." He pulled Hannah with him until they were off by themselves.

Laredo rolled his eyes at Tex. "Did you have to bring him?"

"Oh, well. He can amuse himself now." Tex smiled at Katy. "How've you been, anyway?"

"Just busy. What brings you to Lonely Hearts Station?"

"We came to give Laredo some tip—"

"They just stopped by to say hello," Laredo said.

"It's nice of you to check on your twin. Is it true that twins are really close?" Katy asked.

"No," Laredo said.

Tex laughed. "We're fraternal in mind-set, you might say. I'm the settled one, Laredo is the wild one. If one of us was ever in a fistfight at school, the teachers didn't bother to check which one of us it was. They just automatically called Mason and said, 'Come get Laredo.'"

"It wasn't quite like that," Laredo said, getting more annoyed with his twin by the second. "I wasn't a hooligan."

"I grow roses," Tex said.

"Oh, I love roses," Katy replied.

The dreamy tone in her voice as she stared into his twin's eyes was almost more than Laredo could stomach. Her reaction was the same as every other woman's when Tex mentioned those stupid roses. Clearly, the roses were a conversational prop Tex employed just to get a woman's attention—he probably grew the stupid things just to get on women's good sides. "Okay, enough with the flowery stuff. Can we get on with the lesson?"

"Lesson?" Katy repeated.

"Yeah, I'm teaching Tex everything I know about bulls."

"I thought you didn't know anything," Katy said, her voice innocent.

Tex snickered, and Laredo made a mental note to

punch him later. "I know a few things," he said, trying to hang on to his bravado. Something about Katy just got him so mixed up and confused! He wanted to brag in front of her, wanted to strut his stuff just a little, but somehow he kept goofing it up.

"What Laredo means," Hannah said, as she and Ranger moved back to the circle, "is that he knows more about Bloodthirsty Black. He's filling Tex in on the history."

"That's right." Laredo straightened with a grateful glance at Hannah. "History's important."

"Yeah, we all remember your report card," Ranger said.

Silence descended. "Excuse me," Tex said. "I'm going to go find a gents'."

He left, and the conversational void stretched. Laredo frowned at Ranger, who sighed.

"Now, just what is it about this bull we need to know?" Ranger said, clearly deciding to leave off the sibling rivalry and let Laredo get his neck broken if he was determined to do so.

"He pulls to the left," a voice said. "And then, just when you lean, he jerks to the right with a mean midair kick. Every time."

All four of them whirled to look at the woman who'd spoken. Laredo felt his jaw go slack, and heard Ranger's jaw hit the pavement with a resounding thunk.

This woman was simply stunning. As fresh and cute as Katy was, as punky-funky cute as Hannah was, this woman would set records for head-snapping stares.

Beside him, he could feel Katy stiffen.

"Hell-oo, there," Ranger said. "Thanks for the tip." He tipped his hat to her, and grinned.

The woman smiled back, one hand on her hip, the other casually resting against Bloodthirsty Black's stall. "You're welcome."

Laredo glanced at Katy for an intro. Hannah didn't seem too happy about the woman's presence, either, especially since she and Ranger had just spent a cozy five-minute chat together.

The woman ignored the female frostiness and extended a delicate hand to Ranger. "Staying in town long?" she asked softly, her voice full of hints.

"He's leaving in a couple of hours, actually," Laredo replied.

"And you?" she asked smoothly, looking back to Laredo.

He probably shouldn't tell what he was up to, Laredo thought. Katy probably wanted him to be the surprise weapon. "Uh, a guy can't hang around beautiful women in a quaint town forever, I guess."

"That's too bad. We're real nice to strangers here in Lonely Hearts Station." The woman smiled, and imperceptibly tightened her posture so that her breasts thrust forward in an invitation even the greenest male could understand.

Laredo thought he could see Ranger's eyes spinning around in their sockets. Wow! He didn't think he'd ever seen his hard-edged brother so...softened up.

"This is Cissy Kisserton," Katy said reluctantly. "Cissy, meet Ranger and Laredo Jefferson."

"Real cowboys?" Cissy asked.

"Born and bred, ma'am," Ranger said. Hannah rolled her eyes, which Laredo thought was appropriate.

"Well, I don't want to keep you," Cissy said. "Just wanted to be friendly to the visitors in town. You send them over our way for a cup of cocoa, Katy. We'll make sure they're well taken care of."

"It's a bit chilly in here, after all, isn't it?" Ranger said. "I'll take you up on that cup of cocoa right now, Miss Cissy," he said, following after the beautiful woman like a lovestruck puppy.

The two of them disappeared around the corner, but not before Laredo saw Ranger slip his arm around her. Laughter floated over the stalls to them. Laredo groaned to himself. Ranger was the most steadfast of the brothers! Certainly he had his share of wild hairs—he'd been bluffing about going to do some military service for nearly a year now...of course, he'd never leave Malfunction Junction Ranch, but he'd sure been trying to put action where his big mouth was. He'd actually started hanging around the police station, trying to act civilized.

But nothing like a beautiful woman to make a man's mouth run away from him. Laredo looked at Katy, who appeared dumbfounded; Hannah seemed disappointed down to her very orange toenails, peeping out of cut-open tennis shoes.

The expression on Hannah's face told Laredo that Cissy wasn't the only woman around who thought Ranger was a hunk.

Oh, boy.

"Where's Ranger?" Tex asked, coming back to join them.

"He went off with a woman," Laredo said. "Cissy Kisserton. You should have seen her."

"You should have seen *him*," Hannah said. "It was like watching a giant tree get felled by one termite."

"Oh. I apologize for my brother's behavior," Tex said.

"Is Cissy a Never Lonely Cut-N-Gurl?" Laredo asked.

"Obviously," Katy said.

"Whoa." He'd have to be very careful to avoid that Venus fly trap. There was a real sensitive issue between the two salons for certain, and it clearly wasn't all about who gave the better haircut. "By the way, Tex, Cissy was awfully helpful. She says Bloodthirsty Black pulls to the left. And when you lean, he jerks to the right with a midair kick every time."

"Does he, now?" Tex eyed the bull speculatively. "And why was the competition being so helpful?"

Laredo looked at Katy and Hannah. "I guess she just wanted to be nice to the strangers in town."

Katy and Hannah made disgusted sounds, gathered up their baskets with the food in them and marched off without a word.

The parting looks they shot the men spoke loudly, however.

"You just blew it," Tex told his twin.

"What did I say?"

"First rule of girlhunting—never let a woman you like believe another woman has anything to offer you. Anyway, I'm supposed to be giving you tips on Mr. Bloodthirsty, here, not love. It's unseemly for a brother to have to coach his twin in things any freshly minted teenage boy knows."

Laredo's heart sank. "Cissy was awfully friendly. I thought she was nice. And she didn't have to tell us about the trick this old bull plays."

"True."

"Ranger stuck on her like glue. He didn't see anything wrong with her, either."

"There, then. You don't have anything to worry about."

Laredo frowned. Nothing to worry about except he'd upset Katy, and that was the last thing he wanted to do.

"Pulls to the left, huh?" Tex said. "When I went to the gents', I noticed the arena was empty. There's no one around. Let's sit you up on Bloodthirsty and see exactly how hard he kicks."

"Have you lost your mind? I'm not getting up on him." Laredo eyed the bull, who was pawing at something in his stall as if he were sharpening his hooves for the kill. "Don't we need about four other men helping us hold him?"

"If we were loading him in a chute, yeah. But you're just gonna get up on top of this bull and get used to the feel of him underneath you."

Laredo shook his head. "I'll wait till Saturday."

Tex sighed. "Look. It's not that hard. Watch me."

He pulled on his glove and looped a rope around the bull's neck. The animal snorted, demonstrating his displeasure by slinging his head. Tex jumped up on the top rail, squared himself up, jumped and landed briefly on the bull's back.

There was silence for an infinitesimally split second, and then all hell broke loose.

"I DON'T THINK the Jefferson boys are the men we thought they were," Katy said to Hannah as they walked home. "Laredo brags, Tex is a ladies' man and Ranger's off with the enemy."

Hannah nodded. "For a minute I thought Ranger might have liked me. He sure seemed to."

Katy's heart melted at the sound of sadness in Hannah's voice. "It's just that darn Cissy Kisserton. She knocks men down at their kneecaps."

"But if he'd really liked me, he wouldn't have even seen her," Hannah said. "You notice Laredo didn't so much as shake her hand."

Katy brightened a little. "I suppose he didn't." Then she faded again. "But he's still a braggart. If

I were to fall for another man, I know I'd want one whose actions match his words.''

"That may be the impossible holy grail, Katy. All men pad their résumés. So do women.''

"*I* don't.''

"You *do*,'' Hannah insisted. "I've noticed that since Laredo hit town, you're trying to stand like our competition does. Tush out and breasts stuck forward.''

Together, they walked up the back-stair entrance of the salon and went upstairs to Katy's room. "It's true,'' Katy said. "That's exactly what I was doing. But if I don't shift things around, I'll never stand a chance against a girl like Cissy. She's got all the moves. And it's only a matter of time before those girls set their aim on Laredo. I just don't want to be around when they score a bull's-eye.''

"Now, now.'' Hannah sank onto the bed and stared down at Rose the mouse. "Courage. Laredo seems loftier in morals than most men.''

"I don't know. I noticed a marked decrease in loftiness when Cissy came by. We brought picnic baskets, and Cissy brought a tight skirt and high heels.''

Hannah frowned slightly. "I thought I might like Ranger, but it was one of those moments where you look at someone and see someone they're not because you want them to be something else. I must be in a needy phase. I'll have to be more careful.''

Katy sat beside her, and patted Hannah's hand. "What happened to daring?''

"That's you, not me." Hannah perked up. "Katy, stand up," she said.

Katy complied, her eyes widening when she saw the scissors Hannah picked up from the table. "Not my hair, Hannah," Katy protested. "I know you've been itching to cut it for a long time, but it's unwise to give up an inch for a man. Truly, short and sassy isn't me."

"It is when you've got nice legs you never show," Hannah said, picking up the hem of Katy's long dress. She decisively cut up to Katy's knee.

"Hannah!"

"Hold still, I'm gauging your siren potential. I think another two inches," Hannah murmured, continuing to cut.

"I'm too short for short dresses," Katy protested. "I'll look even more like a baby-faced doll than I do!"

Hannah tossed the red fabric aside. "Nope," she said happily. "Now that's enough to give Laredo whiplash."

"Hannah." Katy knelt down to look into her friend's eyes. "Listen to me. Laredo Jefferson is the last man I need. He doesn't fit the description. In fact, in some ways he reminds me of Stanley."

Hannah cocked a wry brow. "In what ways? Stand back up so I can gauge the hem length."

"Laredo's ogle-meter. And that's enough to tell me that he's not even remotely close to…date material."

"Did Stanley ogle Becky before the two of them met like ships passing in the bridal chamber?"

Katy wrinkled her nose. "Not that I ever noticed. I think that was why I was so shocked."

"Something doesn't add up about that. What made those two suddenly jump in each other's arms?"

"My virginity."

"No." Hannah sighed, pulled out a needle from a drawer in Katy's nightstand and threaded it with red thread. Industriously, she went to work turning up the hem of Katy's dress by an eighth of an inch. "Linen's hard to sew by hand," she murmured. "I'm going to take tiny stitches, so stand very still."

"Don't you need a chalk or tape?"

"This will do for the lunch hour. I need you to concentrate. Did you ever tell Becky anything about Stanley?"

"I told her everything! She was my best friend, my maid of honor."

"Did you tell her anything personal? Like, oh, that you two hadn't slept together?"

"Everybody knew that, even my mother. We had a nine-month proper engagement. Stanley used to say he was proud to be marrying a virgin." She wrinkled her forehead.

"Don't do that. Your face will look like a race track," Hannah instructed.

"I told Becky everything a girl tells her best friend. Just like I tell you. She also knew that Stanley didn't like to kiss me."

Hannah stopped sewing. "What?"

"Stanley didn't like to kiss me. Why are you looking at me like that?"

Hannah shook her head. "Why didn't he?"

"He said it was too much temptation, since we couldn't...um, you know."

"And Stanley's family is wealthy?"

"Right. Stanley Peter St. Collin III, of St. Collin Faucets and Hinges."

"Oh, of course. Naturally." Hannah grimaced. "And Becky's family was where on the social register?"

"Well, way below ours, if you must use social register terms. Her mom and dad divorced a long time ago, when she was a child. And her mom worked as a waitress at night to make ends meet. Becky worked two jobs, too, after we graduated from high school."

"And your parents were the Goodnights of Goodnight Protective Arms, starting with well-heeled British immigrant parents and going back three pedigreed generations in your hometown. And you dutifully and impressively went to college and obtained a degree in chemistry."

"Well, it was the easiest thing to do," Katy said. "Chemistry is much easier than economics or something." She shuddered. "Columns of figures and business principles, or putting cool stuff like hydrogen chloride into test tubes and seeing what blows up. Protons. Dissection. No contest there, huh?"

"Oh, yeah. I can see where chemistry is the easy

answer. Miles and miles of chemical configurations.'' Hannah went back to sewing.

"After I sort myself out—and I'm just about done, thanks to Miss Delilah—I'm going to teach chemistry at Duke in North Carolina in the fall. Of course, my original plan was to marry Stanley and become a perfectly manicured, Mrs. St. Collin III. Luckily, I'd sent out lots of applications after I graduated from college and *before* Stanley proposed. He didn't like me interviewing at Duke. Did I tell you that I was invited to interview at Cornell, too?''

"Peachy. Turn.'' Hannah moved the needle in and out without glancing up. "These pretty legs are wasted on a chem prof.

"So, Duke in the fall.''

"Yes.'' Katy sighed. "I should never have given up chemical calculations for a man.''

"Not Stanley, anyway. But you can't throw marriage overboard and closet yourself in a lab.''

"Look at me, Hannah, please.''

Hannah complied, and Katy smiled at her friend.

"You have all been wonderful to me. But it's time for me to strike out on my own and realize my true potential. I'm not man savvy. I'm not sophisticated. I spent too many years studying while my girlfriends were hanging out at frat houses to have learned the feminine ropes. If life is based on sexual chemistry, I got an F in the sexual and an A plus in the chemistry. But being smart means I can take care of myself. I think I might have gotten a little nervous about my life, and when Stanley proposed, I jumped at it. Maybe I didn't want to be the smartest virgin spinster.'' She sighed, looking down for just a moment. ''In a way, Stanley dumping me at the altar was the best thing that could have happened. It made me realize I'm much safer if I just rely on myself.''

Hannah shook her head. ''I think if you hadn't told Becky that Stanley didn't like to kiss you, she still would have stolen him. She needed a way out of her life, and you only thought you did. I think you subconsciously gave her the invitation to steal him.''

Katy stared into the mirror, seeing the miracle Hannah had wrought with her dress. She looked like a different person. Sexier. Hipper. ''Maybe I had some unconscious motive I didn't recognize, but I wouldn't have picked my wedding day to be dumped.''

''That was unfortunate, but she was probably plagued by guilt, which caused her to wait until the last minute to act. She's probably not enjoying her honeymoon at all, thinking about you crying your eyes out.'' Hannah stood. ''I haven't seen you cry at all, Katy. And I think all this talk of sexual dysfunction is a cover-up. Maybe you just wanted to keep men on the periphery of your life.''

''If I didn't then, I do now. It's humiliating when the maid of honor marries your fiancé, wearing the hot pink dress you picked out for her. It's like, here's hot and sexy and here's plain and virginal. Which do you think most guys want? *I* don't know,'' Katy murmured. ''You sure have a lot of insight into people, Hannah. How did you develop that?''

"I'm a hairdresser. I've heard lots of stories over the years. Be still." Gently she took hold of Katy's below-shoulder-length hair, slicked it into a smooth, high ponytail, then took one strand which she wound around the rubber band and pinned down. "Now a touch of red lipstick," she said, applying it to Katy as she spoke, "and whammo! Instant femme fatale."

Katy inspected herself in the mirror. "Maybe it's fatal femininity."

"Think confident. Be confident. *I'm* confident that you're a woman not to be overlooked. Anyway, the plain-vanilla you is all but a memory." Satisfied, Hannah put away the needle and thread and the hairbrush and lipstick, glancing with cool smugness at Katy's dress. "See how easy it is to be daring?"

"This is daring?"

"For you? Yes. It's a start. Let's go have lunch at the cafeteria, Virginity Barbie. All this thinking's made me hungry."

LAREDO HESITATED outside the door of the Never Lonely Cut-N-Gurls Salon. If Katy saw him going in here, he was toast. Unfortunately, he needed Ranger, and he needed him *now*.

Glancing guiltily across the street at the Lonely Hearts Salon, he pushed open the door.

KATY GASPED as she saw Laredo go inside the enemy camp. She and Hannah stepped back inside the door quickly, staring at each other in surprise.

"Whoa," Hannah said. "I have to admit to being caught off guard."

Katy's heart felt as if it bled a drop as red as her newly short dress. "I told you. It's a dysfunctional thing. Those girls have allure—and I do not." Why should she even care? she asked herself. She didn't like him anyway.

Did she?

"Boys will be boys, I suppose," Hannah said. "You could go rescue him from himself."

"I'd rather join Marvella's payroll. Come on. Let's go eat at the cafeteria. Only, we're taking the back door. I wouldn't dream of allowing Mr. I'll-Ride-That-Bull-For-You to know we saw him slinking into the competition's bunker."

Chapter Four

"Hold still, Tex," Ranger said, his teeth gritted, slightly annoyed at being dragged away from Cissy to tend his brother in Delilah's barn. Tex was writhing a bit dramatically on the hay-covered floor, and Ranger had been far more impressed with the shoulder-massage Cissy had been giving him back at the salon atop a satin-covered chaise lounge. "I've got to check your shoulder good because if it's broken, it'll set crooked. What were you thinking, anyway?"

Tex tried his hardest to lie still while Ranger none too gently probed his back and shoulder. "I wanted to test this bull and see if what Cissy said was true."

Laredo stared at his prone twin. "You couldn't tell a darn thing with that bull in a pen."

"I can tell you he's got a helluva liftoff. But I don't think he cranks left. No, I don't."

Ranger stopped what he was doing to look at his brother. "You don't think he cranks left?"

Tex shook his head. "I don't."

The three men studied the bull through the rails.

Bloodthirsty seemed satisfied to have flung Tex into the stall across the aisle. For the moment he was quite a bit calmer.

"He does have a spring-loaded midair jump, though," Tex said. "Either this bull's changed his mind about how he tries to kill people or you were getting set up, Laredo."

Ranger shook his head. "Cissy's a nice girl. She wouldn't deliberately tell someone wrong."

"And bulls don't change their mind," Tex said stubbornly. "If they start out kicking left, that's usually the way they always go. Bloodthirsty didn't hesitate. Then he bunched himself up in the air and tossed me over the pen."

Laredo wasn't certain what to think. "Why would Cissy give me a bad tip?"

"So you'd lose, dummy," Tex told him. "She's a woman, and she's a rival, and she's sucking Ranger's face to make certain all her bases are covered."

"She didn't suck my face!" Ranger protested.

"Your lips are pink," Laredo pointed out. "Did you borrow some tinted chapstick, maybe? Drink a strawberry pop? Borrow a sun lamp and use it on your lips?"

"It was just a friendly peck," Ranger said. "Nothing more." But his face and neck turned as pink as the lipstick, and Laredo frowned.

"Why are you lying?"

"I'm not." Ranger shrugged and gently helped

Tex to his feet. "I think your shoulder's fine. Just don't test him again anytime soon."

"Why? So we won't interrupt your friendly pecking with Cissy?" Tex asked. "What's gotten into you?"

"What's gotten into you?" Ranger shot back. "Since when have you cared who I talked to?"

"Since we're supposed to be here helping out a woman who rescued us last month, Ranger," Laredo stated. "Have you forgotten whose girls helped us and Union Junction through the big storm? Who helped with sandbagging, and cooking, and mopping up a creek's worth of water? Who hung curtains in our house and cleaned and generally kept the town from getting washed under?"

Ranger stared at his brothers, speechless. He shook his head as if his ears were buzzing. Then his shoulders drooped. "I don't know what came over me," he said, his tone apologetic. "It was like…it was like the call of the wild, and I couldn't shut it off. Like being in a dream I didn't want to wake up from." He looked at them sheepishly. "For a minute there, I was almost totally hypnotized by a woman. Whew!"

"Oh, boy." Tex shook his head. "Listen, we've got to keep our heads on straight. Our brother has signed on to ride one of the worst bulls I've ever come in contact with, and he has no idea what he's doing. We've gotta have a plan."

"My plan is to get on and stay on," Laredo said. "I'm going to be more stubborn than this bull."

Bloodthirsty Black cared little for Laredo's announcement. He gave a round-nostriled snort, reminding everyone he was in the business of tossing cowboys as if they were hay.

"Maybe you should just give money to Miss Delilah's charity," Ranger said doubtfully.

"It's a man thing." Laredo glanced toward the barn exit. "In Spain, they run from bulls. Malfunction Junction Ranch cowboys laugh in the face of danger."

"And get gored," Tex said narrowly. "Are you falling for Katy Goodnight? Did something happen last month we don't know about?"

"Nope. Nothing went on between us except some mopping and some curtain hanging."

Ranger and Tex looked at each other. "Oh," they said in unison.

"What? What does that mean?" Laredo asked suspiciously.

"Keeping house," Tex explained. "The two of you were trying on domesticity. And you must have liked it."

"We were not! And I didn't!" He glanced around to make certain Katy hadn't decided to return unexpectedly—although, he figured that was hoping for too much. He lowered his voice. "But when she mops, she really moves her tush. Man, oh, man. That's what I remember most about her!"

Tex and Ranger groaned. "I'm sure she'd love to hear that," his twin said. "We'll pull together and buy her a bottle of Mop & Glo for a wedding gift."

"She can mop up your blood when this bull's done with you," Ranger said, equally disgusted. "You dummy."

BOTH HIS BROTHERS had called him a dummy, but Laredo didn't care. Something was telling him that this was the right moment in his life to do A Big Thing. This was his time to shine. And he couldn't wait.

His brothers left in disgust to go find a hamburger, but he wanted to find Katy. He headed over to the Lonely Hearts Salon, only to be told she'd gone to the Lonely Hearts Station Cafeteria with Hannah.

Waving his thanks, he loped off in that direction, quickly passing by the Never Lonely Cut-N-Gurls Salon without a glance.

The blinds snapped back into place in an upstairs room when he strode by.

"THAT'S THE COWBOY you were supposed to bring back, Cissy. Not that Ranger one."

"I wasn't expecting there to be two cowboys, and they both fit your description," Cissy explained. "But Ranger's a good kisser. It certainly wasn't time wasted."

"You wasted my time," Marvella insisted. "Three days before the rodeo. We need to turn Katy's cowboy to our way of thinking. I want you to try again."

Cissy smiled. "With these men, it's a pleasure.

But he seems to like Katy very well. What if he won't be lured into our salon?''

"You are my magic potion, my dear. No man has ever looked in your eyes and said no. I'm confident you'll be up to the job."

She peeked at the cowboy, who was heading at a near jog toward the cafeteria. "But what *if?*"

"If the *what if* happens—and I don't believe you have a failure rate anywhere in that man-magnet body of yours—we'll simply kidnap him the night before. Just like we did the last cowboy."

Cissy laughed. "That was so much fun. It was like having our own cowboy toy for the night."

"If you're hungry, Cissy, I'll buy your lunch at the cafeteria."

Cissy put out her hand, palm up. "I'm always hungry."

"DON'T LOOK NOW, but here comes your cowboy," Hannah said. "Be nice to him, please, Katy? He looks anxious."

Katy gave Laredo a brief smile as he sat down next to them.

"Hi, Katy," he said.

"Hi, Laredo. I forgot to ask you how you slept last night? Good?" She was all prepared to act as if she'd never thought about liking this cowboy. Stiff and formal—and nothing more than acquaintances.

"I did. Thanks for letting me sleep in your room. How did you sleep in Delilah's room?"

"Very well. Thanks for asking."

And that was all she could think of to say, because she really wanted to ask him why he'd gone over to the Never Lonely Salon. That would break the acquaintances' rule of no prying, though.

"Hi, Hannah," Laredo said.

"Hey. Get your bull all figured out?"

"I think so, but I missed getting to eat what you two had in those picnic baskets."

He looked at Katy when he said this, and she felt herself flush because she'd flounced off in a snit over Cissy Kisserton.

"So…were your brothers any help?"

"Tex is. He knows more than just about any of us about bulls."

"I can't tell the two of you apart," Hannah said. "Do you ever have trouble when you go places?"

"Nah. I'm nicer than he is. More outgoing. People notice."

Katy stared at him. "I don't know if I agree that you're the more outgoing of the two."

He smiled and slid his hand over to snag a French fry off her plate. "Tex is always thinking about ratios of manure versus fertilizer composition, et cetera."

"Ratios?" Hannah perked up.

"Yeah. And the chemical configurations of fertilizer and exciting things like that. Real exciting."

"Maybe you set your sights on the wrong twin," Hannah murmured, but Katy kicked her underneath the table. Then, embarrassed because Laredo had heard, she excused herself to go get another glass of lemonade.

For the first time in her life, men's heads turned as she walked to the soda fountain. She hoped Laredo was watching. She hoped he realized she could be as sexy as a girl like Cissy—she'd just needed a little coaching—and she walked a little more slowly to give him time to notice, in case he was slow on the uptake. She smiled at a stranger in a pair of jeans and what looked like an expensive Italian shirt. Why anyone would wear an Italian shirt in Lonely Hearts Station, she didn't know, but his ponytail was as long as hers only not so high on his head. To her surprise, he got up from his table and began walking toward her.

Uh-oh, she thought. She'd gone and done it now! Her sexy short dress was one thing, but piling on confidence she didn't have and a big smile might have—

"Excuse me," the man said as she busily tried to get the soda fountain to work. For some reason it wouldn't pour the lemonade!

"Yes?" she asked nervously, forcing herself to look at him. After all, Laredo was watching, and he'd just been in the enemy camp, and two could play at that game. Right! If only she could get through this moment, she'd go home and take her silly ponytail down and put on one of her long dresses.

"I'm Lars Van Hooven from *Playboy Magazine,*" he said, handing her a card, which she hesitantly took from him. "Photographer. We've been combing the United States for small-town girls for our magazine."

"Playboy Magazine?" Her head was spinning. Why would he be giving her a card?

"Yes," he said with a smile that definitely wasn't wolfish. It was a smile meant to comfort her. "We're going to do a pictorial on small-town girls, and you've definitely got what we're looking for."

"Oh, thank you," Katy said, not certain exactly what she had.

"If you want to try out for the magazine, we'd fly you to our offices, all expenses paid."

She tried to hand the card back. "Well, Mr. uh, Mr. Lars, I'm not really—"

"I know," he said with another easy, winning smile. "It's okay. Keep the card. Think it over. Call me if you have any questions. Maybe you'll change your mind. I live for girls who change their minds."

"I see. Okay, well, thank you."

"You're welcome." He reached above her, flipped the lemonade switch, and, magically, her cup filled. In her nervousness, she hadn't pressed the switch properly.

She felt her face flush. "Thank you," she said, her smile shy and embarrassed.

"Magical," he said, staring at her. "Please change your mind about calling me."

And then he walked away. Katy looked back at her cup, which now sparkled with lemonade. Never, she thought. No way.

But she *was* going to have Hannah cut off every dress in her closet!

She tucked the card into her purse when she sat down.

"What did that guy want?" Laredo asked.

"He just helped me get the lemonade working," Katy said with an innocent smile. "Laredo, you haven't told us about your family. How are they doing?"

"Well, we still have the housekeeper from hell. Helga keeps everyone on a rigid schedule and drives us all nuts, but Mason would get rid of us before he got rid of her. He believes she hung the curtains you hung, and stocked his freezer with casseroles, so we're stuck with her. And he's too tore up to notice any different, because Mimi's getting married to a city slicker, and Mason's too proud to hunt her down and make her change her mind."

Hannah ate some Jell-O. "Maybe it's a family trait. Those are the worst to break. So...where's Tex?"

And Ranger, Katy knew she wanted to say.

"My brothers went to get a hamburger. I came to see how y'all were doing."

He gave Katy a smile that said, See? I'm different from Mason. I'm not too proud to hunt down a woman. "I like your dress, Katy."

He'd noticed! And after he'd been to the opposing camp, too. Actually, he hadn't stayed long, now that she thought about it...and he wasn't wearing any lipstick stains. He hadn't backed out of riding

Bloodthirsty Black. And he didn't smell like perfume, just warm male. Slowly she smiled back at him, feeling her whole face relax as she decided to forgive him for taking a detour.

Across the cafeteria a camera whirred, snapping up pictures of a small-town girl on the verge of falling in love with her cowboy.

CISSY WALKED into the Lonely Hearts Station Cafeteria, seeing the same beatific, early-crush smile the camera was enjoying.

She had to work fast, that was for certain. Marvella never fired anyone, but when things didn't work her way, she could be a witch on a broom and make a woman's life miserable for weeks.

She ran a quick hand over her platinum, show-stopping locks and smoothed her miniskirt. Then she started walking, the way a woman walks when she's got a destination in mind.

"Hello, Laredo," she said, leaning over to move in between Katy and him. She gave him a fast kiss on the cheek he couldn't get away from. "We really enjoyed seeing you at our place. Come on by... anytime."

Stunned into a grin, he looked up at Cissy, not missing, Katy noticed, her full-size breasts on the way to her eyes.

"We'd invite you to sit down," Laredo said, his manners in full effect, "but there's no room."

"Oh, I'd lo-o-ove to sit with you-all," she said silkily, and nudged Katy over with a hip. "Katy, honey, scoot over. You're hogging the bench."

Chapter Five

Cissy sank onto the bench between Laredo and Katy, giving him a dazzling smile and an eyeful of cleavage as she sat. She sure smelled good—and her platinum locks brushed his bare arm. His mouth dried out.

What was it Ranger had said? He'd suddenly heard the call of the wild? Blinking to chase off the pea-soup inertia taking over his brain—which curiously came accompanied by a sound like horns warning ships to stay clear during dense fog—Laredo tore his gaze away from Cissy. He looked across the table at Hannah, who was staring at him curiously, her spoonful of quivering red Jell-O, halfway to her mouth. Like a drowning man, he focused on Hannah's direct gaze and her wild and tousled hairdo and pulled his brain out of the drowning swirl it was caught in.

He might not have ever ridden a bull, but he knew when he was set directly on the horns of a dilemma. "Hannah," he said, slowly and carefully, shutting his ears to the call of the wild, "would you mind keeping Miss Cissy company? I'm going to walk Katy back to the salon because she needs to feed Rose."

"Feed…oh, oh, sure," Hannah said, catching on. "I'll be happy to, Laredo."

"Please excuse us, Miss Cissy," Laredo said, nodding to her as he took his tray and Katy's. "We'll be seeing you around."

Katy said goodbye to Hannah and Cissy, seeming more than happy to leave.

"I hope you don't mind," Laredo said as they walked out into the bright sunlight. "You looked like you were done eating."

She smiled up at him. "I was happy to go."

"Good."

"Rose was an inventive excuse."

"It was the truth. Since I slept in your room last night, I didn't figure you'd had a chance to feed her. I picked her up out of her box, and she told me she wasn't the kind of girl to be handled before she'd had her breakfast."

Katy smiled, and he looked at her appreciatively. "You look real nice, Katy."

"Thank you." She hesitated before glancing up at him. "Laredo, are you sure you're all right with riding Bloodthirsty Black?"

"I want to do it. It's a personal issue for me, a goal I've set for myself."

"Goals are good."

"What are your goals?"

"To be a first-rate chemistry professor at Duke in the fall," she murmured.

"Chemistry. I like chemistry," he said, cupping her face with one hand.

"Really?" she asked.

"Unless Tex is talking about it. Then it has something to do with flowers and is annoying."

"Some women like flowers," she said on a breath as he stroked her cheek and then her chin.

"Tex's flowers never mature," Laredo told her. "They never get from bud to bloom. I prefer a more direct process for my goals."

"Like, get on mad beefsteak, get neck broken by mad beefsteak?" she asked with a smile.

"Something like that."

"You're doing this out of a sense of responsibility. If I hadn't dragged you into our salon, you'd be halfway to— Where were you going, anyway?"

"Anywhere," he said, leaning down to place his lips gently on hers. "Somewhere," he murmured, as he felt her still beneath him. "Probably nowhere as fun as Lonely Hearts Station."

Then he kissed Katy the way he'd been wanting to since he'd first noticed her tush when she was mopping.

And when he felt her unstiffen, felt her relax against him and then felt her lips move under his, Laredo decided Katy was even better at kissing than mopping.

"SORRY THAT DIDN'T WORK OUT for you," Hannah said gleefully. "Guess your sexual grenades don't get Laredo's attention. Maybe he's more the subtle type. You know, sparklers instead of incendiary devices.''

''I wouldn't say that. He ran out of here for a reason.'' Cissy smiled with surety. ''A man only runs when he's afraid.''

''I'd be afraid of you, too, Cissy.''

Cissy tapped Hannah's tray with a fingernail. ''Pay attention here, country girl. He's afraid of being *tempted*.''

''Oh, was that what made him run?'' Hannah finished up her Jell-O and licked the spoon with smug contentment. ''Temptation. Hmm. Remind me never to try that on a man.''

Cissy leaned forward. ''Hannah, you may think you were working a direct angle with your little blueberry napkin-lined basket, but you saw how quickly *Ranger* did whatever I wanted.''

The smugness left Hannah's face.

''Yes, Hannah, dear, one of us has kissed him, and the other has not.''

Hannah sat very still, watching Cissy with big eyes.

''So if I were you, I'd not be too quick with the congratulations to Katy.'' Cissy stood. ''I have only just begun. Besides, I melted Ranger easily enough. Why shouldn't his brother be just as easy?''

''Is there a reason you can't confine yourself to Ranger?'' Hannah said, though it hurt like heck to say it.

"There is a reason, and it's really none of your business," Cissy said, her voice biting enough to make Hannah sit up straight.

"Can't your salon win without cheating?"

"It's not cheating if your cowboys always fall apart at the last second."

And yet it would take a man of iron not to fall for Cissy and the Never Lonely girls. They just knew what it took to wind a man's sex drive into full gear. Poor Katy didn't have a chance against them. "Why does Marvella hate Delilah so much?" Hannah asked.

"I'm only an employee," Cissy said with a toss of her beautiful hair. "I do what I'm told, and I make a good living. Can you say the same?"

"Well, we're not performing the same tasks," Hannah retorted. "So I don't think we can compare paychecks. Cissy, do you think, just this once, you could leave a man alone? I think Katy really likes Laredo, and she's just getting over a broken heart."

"One never pulls back just when they're about to win the war."

"Excuse me, ladies," a man's voice interrupted. "Lars Van Hooven, photographer for *Playboy Magazine*."

"*Playboy Magazine!*" Cissy said, lighting up like morning sunshine. "I'm Cissy. How do you do?"

"Fine, thanks." Lars glanced away from her to look at Hannah. "I met your friend over by the soda fountain, and I gave her a business card in case she decided to try out for our small-town girls pictorial.

But I forgot her name. Can you tell me what it was?"

"Katy Goodnight," Hannah said with a pointed smile for Cissy. "Although I hate to dim your hopes, but I don't think you'll be hearing from her. Katy's a shy, innocent kind of girl. A real diamond among bad fakes."

Cissy stuck her tongue out at Hannah. Hannah winked back.

"Thanks for the info." He tapped Katy's name into a Palm Pilot, missing the byplay between the two women. "She's exactly what we're looking for."

"Need a blonde?" Cissy asked, all her charm on display.

Lars shook his head as he put his organizer away. "Sorry. Thanks for offering. But what we have in mind is freshness, and that country sweetness. The world is really looking for innocence right now." He nodded to them and left.

"Well, well, well," Hannah said. "Totally immune to you."

"Only because he's gay, Hannah. I never said I could work miracles," Cissy snapped.

"Freshness and country sweetness. Can you say *defeated,* Cissy? This war is lost."

"We'll see on Saturday, won't we?" Cissy gave her a shriveling glare and stalked away.

THE SENSATION of being thoroughly kissed by Laredo had Katy turned inside out. Everything in her body felt weak and somehow shaky, feelings she'd never felt before.

It was too much, too powerful, too soon. Her heart had been betrayed last month, by her best friend and her fiancé. Nothing that felt this overwhelmingly hot and passionate could be taken slow and easy.

She felt as if she was standing square on the point of no return, and in serious danger of falling over the edge. Parts of her body she'd never known could react felt as if they were filling with liquid fire.

Before she could help herself, she pulled away from Laredo, blinking up at him in wonder.

"What's wrong, sweetheart?" he asked.

"I...I don't know," she said on a gasp. "I've never been kissed like that before."

He smiled. "Then let's do it again and go for two."

But this was no light matter for her. Pieces of her had flown out of their usual reserved place, like glass chips missing from a window. She felt fragile in his arms, when she needed to be getting stronger. *Sweetheart?* Not her. "I'm sorry," she said quickly. "Laredo...I'm not the girl for you."

And then she ran into the Lonely Hearts Salon.

Laredo scratched his head as he watched Katy flee. Not the girl for him? Of course she wasn't the girl for him. He wasn't looking for a girl to be right for him. He was passing through town on his way to big things, whatever it was that he could pit his strength and his smarts against.

This stop in Lonely Hearts Station was just Big Thing #1.

Of course he liked Katy, liked her an awful lot. Wouldn't want to hurt her.

And yet, he understood what she was saying. She didn't want to be played fast and loose. She wasn't available for a good time.

Fact was, she was right. Neither he nor any of his brothers had ever itched to be settled. Frisco Joe getting caught was a weird thing, but it had shown all the brothers that extra caution was called for or they'd all end up with a wife and a wailing baby.

Of course, Frisco was pretty dang happy.

Laredo thought about his father, who hadn't been seen in years. He thought about his mother, whom he remembered mopping, cleaning, cheerfully making a home and a family with a rough man who'd adored her.

His dad hadn't been able to stand it when the only gentle, sweet flower in his life died. He'd left Mason to raise a houseful of rowdy boys because the pain had been too great.

And that could happen to him if he wasn't careful.

Katy was right: she wasn't the woman for him. There would never be a woman for him.

He should never have kissed her.

He stepped off the curb to head toward the barn to find his brothers, whistling "On the Road Again."

"Hi, Laredo," he heard Cissy Kisserton say as he reached the middle of the narrow street.

"Hey, Cissy." Now there was a woman who wouldn't ask for more than he could give. Nor did he particularly care to give her anything, but there were girls one played around with because they understood the game, and other girls one married.

The kind of girl who understood the rules was eminently more fun, or at least had been before he met Katy. Not the girl for him? In spite of his agreement with her tidy statement, he was puzzled. Somehow Katy had hurt his feelings, and he briefly wondered if he was talking bravado through his cowboy hat.

"Laredo," Cissy said with sweetly downcast eyes as she stood close to him, putting one hand on his T-shirt, "I have a confession to make."

"A confession?" The hairs on the back of his neck seemed to stand up. Something about this woman had a very strange effect on him. It was like watching lightning dance across the sky and wondering if it might strike you if you stood in a wide-open field. He'd not seen Cissy when she wasn't one hundred percent *on,* but right now she had her switch on low wattage, no radiance, dimmed to pleasing supplication.

"Yes," she said softly, finally looking up at him with hugely aquamarine eyes, "Laredo, I'm afraid I lied to you about Bloodthirsty Black."

Chapter Six

At Malfunction Junction Ranch, there were also some untruths being suffered. All the Jefferson brothers seemed painfully aware of the sidestepping, reality-avoiding situation—except one.

Mason sent a glance around the table, eyeing his younger brothers. All present and accounted for, except Frisco Joe, who was in the Texas wine country with Annabelle and baby Emmie, and Laredo, Tex and Ranger, who were goofing off, best as he could tell.

Laredo and his crazy something-big plan. All Mason needed now was another catastrophe to hit, and he'd move out himself.

The front door opened and Mimi Cannady blew in, wearing jeans, a fluffy white sweater and a bright smile to match her new engagement ring. "Hey, everybody!"

Mason instantly lost his appetite. Diamond engagement rings seemed to have that effect on him, or maybe it was just Mimi's two-carat princess-style cut, as she'd described it to him. She'd seemed delighted with it, but he'd been unimpressed. What was he supposed to say: Gee, that's the prettiest ring I ever saw? "Hi, Mimi," he muttered along with his brothers, carefully avoiding glancing at her and her ring.

"Brought you some frozen key-lime pie." She laid it on the table. "Where's everybody else?"

"Gone to make jackasses of themselves," Mason said sourly.

"More so than usual?" she asked, seating herself at the table in the seat that Laredo would have occupied, which just happened to be next to Mason. He could smell her perfume, and it smelled different to him than it had before.

No. It *was* different. "Did you change perfumes?" he demanded.

Mimi and his brothers gawked at him—and then Mimi smiled, bigger than he'd ever seen her smile. "I wouldn't have thought you'd notice such a thing, Mason."

"I noticed because I don't like it," he said hurriedly, though he really did.

Her smile flew off her face, and all his brothers scowled at him.

"You look real nice, Mimi," Calhoun said.

"And you got a new sweater," Last offered. "White looks nice on you, and it's so soft."

"Thank you for the pie," Bandera said. "We're not gonna share with Mason 'cause he's a horse's patoot."

She laughed. "So, where are the Jefferson boys who are making donkeys of themselves?"

"They're in Lonely Hearts Station. Laredo's entered in a rodeo this weekend. He's going to ride a bull named Bloodthirsty Black," Archer said, to a round of chuckles.

"A bull? Laredo can't ride," she said, glancing at Mason.

"He's making a fool of himself for a woman, on the pretext of noble intentions," Mason said.

"Remember the Lonely Hearts ladies who helped us out so much?" Last said. "They needed a cowboy for a charity ride, so Laredo offered. But we think he's really trying to impress Katy Goodnight."

"Oh, that's so sweet!" Mimi glanced at Mason. "That's not being a jackass, Mason. That's *romance*."

He shrugged.

Last sighed. "I'll get a knife for your pie, Mimi. Stay and have a bite with us, will you?"

"No, I've got to get back to Dad," she said, quickly standing. "You *are* all planning to come to my wedding next month, aren't you? It wouldn't feel right not to have all my brothers there."

Every head nodded—except Mason's.

"We wouldn't miss it, Mimi," Last assured her.

"Mason?" she asked softly.

He held back the sigh that begged his chest to heave for release. His jaw locked to keep the words inside him, whatever they might have been. But this was no time for spontaneity. This moment called for…realization.

Things had changed. Everything around him was changing, and it was all out of his control. The days when he was the captain seemed to have evaporated.

Still, a man went down with his ship.

"I'll be there," he said, a lukewarm response that was more a grunt than a promise.

"Thank you." She glanced at him one last time, but he didn't look at her. "Goodbye, fellas. I'll stop by, maybe tomorrow, and check on you. You all are going to see Laredo ride, aren't you?"

They seemed perplexed by that.

"He is your brother. And he very well may need last rites, for heaven's sake," she pointed out. "Of course, love is a wonderful cause to throw caution to the wind for."

The brothers sat silently, although Mason became very interested in the seal on the pepper shaker.

"I reckon we'll go," Last said. "Wanna go with?"

She beamed. "I thought you wouldn't ask. I will, thanks!" And then she left, the wind catching the door as she blew out, causing a noisy slam.

Silence descended after that. Mason could feel his brothers' gazes on him. They didn't need to tell him he'd been cantankerous and mean. He knew it. He just didn't know how else to be around Mimi. Her getting engaged had stopped him cold, shocking him beyond words. In his mind, she'd always been *his* best friend. She was his troublemaker, his life of the party. If there was some fun to be had, she knew how to find it, while he had no more clue about absurd hijinks than a schoolteacher. In a life that had early met hard responsibility, Mimi's spirit had been his let-off valve.

He'd never imagined another fella in the picture.

But suddenly there was, and he was torn. Worse still, though he'd been prepared to dislike the city-slick lawyer in the fancy red sports car, Mason had found that he liked Brian O'Flannigan. He seemed just right for Mimi, a fact that annoyed Mason but which he also admired, when he forced his conscience to be objective.

His brothers got up to leave, taking the pie with them. Mason barely noticed. He sat at the head of the table, staring at nothing, thinking about things he really didn't want to think about, mainly abandonment.

First his mother. Then his father.

Now Mimi.

It was, for reasons he couldn't fathom, the deepest cut he'd ever suffered. No fun at all.

"HI, DAD," Mimi said to Sheriff Cannady as she walked inside the kitchen of their home. "You're up now."

"I am." He smiled at his only child. "You look pretty, honey."

"Thank you." She kissed the top of his head and pulled out another refrigerated key-lime pie. "Your favorite."

Her father smiled, but his skin seemed grayer than it had yesterday. She was worried about him, more worried than she would tell him or anybody else. There was nothing that could be done about it, of course. Her father needed a liver transplant, and the list was long, the chances slim to none. They'd told no one in Union Junction, specifically because her father wanted to go out being the strong sheriff the people had elected for nearly twenty years running. She thought he had a right to that.

They had faced tough odds before. It had always been the two of them against the world.

She couldn't face the thought of losing her father.

Time had run out for her, forcing her to grow up. Mason wouldn't understand that an hourglass didn't have forever to be turned over and over again, keeping the sand pouring continually, infinitely.

If it had been up to her, Mimi knew she would have waited forever for Mason.

Yet even she knew that forever was exactly how long she would have waited—because Mason would never have asked her to marry him. Mason didn't love her. In his mind she would always be the ragamuffin next door, the little girl in ponytails who hung around him like a fun, colorful pest.

Her father's illness had changed her priorities. She couldn't wait any longer for a dream that would never come true. Like the best of fortunes, Brian O'Flannigan had come to help her father with some legal work and fallen head-over-heels in love with her.

It had felt so good to have someone fall for her, someone to want her so much that they were willing to give her half of themselves and so much more. Still, she loved Mason, even though she knew he wasn't capable of loving her the way Brian did. A choice had to be made: she could be happy, or she could be sad.

Strange how her father's life had made her choice easy.

Because if she was going to lose her other parent, the one who'd raised her and loved her with all his heart, she was determined that he was going to see his only child happily married.

And, if God heard her prayers, she was going to make her father a grandfather before he died. He was going to know his grandchild.

She was not prepared to let him go without seeing him hold her baby.

These were the odds she was up against, and Mimi had a well-deserved reputation for being a fighter. This was a battle she meant to win.

"MAYBE IT'S TOO MUCH to ask of Laredo," Delilah said to Jerry the truck driver, who stopped into the salon every time he was near Lonely Hearts Station. They'd become friends and a bit more, in the last month, since he'd driven her and all her girls home from their trip to Union Junction.

Delilah enjoyed having a man around to talk to. Heaven only knew, her sister, Marvella, had stolen every other man in town. But Jerry was more than just male company; he'd become a champion in her corner, and she desperately needed that right now. Picking stubbornly at the letters on a western shirt, Delilah pulled out the name of Lonely Hearts' last champion who'd never even worn the shirt. "Maybe we should let Laredo off the hook and find another cowboy. Laredo barely knows the right end of the bull to hang on to."

Jerry shrugged. "He offered."

"So did you, but I turned you down." She smiled sweetly at the man who reminded everyone of a jolly Santa Claus.

"Because I'm old and fat. That bull wouldn't be able to lift his weight with me on him." Jerry winked at her. "I say turnabout is fair play, anyway. They shanghaied our rider. What do you say we do the same to theirs?"

Delilah laughed. "I don't think I can bring myself to cheat, no matter how much fun it would be."

"Did you know that Cissy Kisserton's out in the middle of the street talking to your cowboy right now?" Jerry asked, staring out the window.

Delilah jumped up from her chair and flew to the window. "That she-devil!"

He shook his head. "Of course, Marvella figures it worked so well last time, why not give it a go again."

"Well, I'll be!" She looked at Jerry. "Gosh, it's not like we have the best of chances since our cowboy's unproven!"

"Our own virgin cowboy," Jerry agreed. "Does

seem like Marvella works just a little too hard at what should be a friendly way to benefit charities.''

''Maybe I'll change my mind about cheating!''

He chuckled and kissed her cheek. ''No one could blame you if you did, but I'd rather see you stick to the honest side.''

She was silent for a minute, weighing her doubts. ''Jerry, I've already let half my girls go. They were lucky. They're settling in Union Junction and opening their own shop. Katy and these other ten gals might not be so fortunate if I have to close up totally. Then how am I going to feel?''

''Like you did the best you could, honey. No one's guaranteed a cakewalk in this life. You gave them fresh starts. Gave them what you had to give. If we get beat, me and you, we're going ice-fishing in Delaware. Or Canada. For good.''

She heard the ''we'' and felt so much better. And yet—

''Jerry, this shop is all mine. It's all I've ever had. When my husband died, I scraped for every penny. Then Marvella's husband left her and we fell in love and got married. I did not steal him,'' Delilah said with a steely eye. ''Marvella has made me the scapegoat, but it was two years after they split up before I even saw her husband.'' She sighed, the memories hard. ''And then he passed away. After that, I was tired of burying husbands. I opened this shop, and it's given me everything I've needed for the past ten years. More than anything, I've enjoyed the girls. They come here sad and hurting, and they get well, and they go away healed. And I'm darn proud of that.''

"But you wouldn't want to kidnap some hapless bull rider just to win."

"I think I would!"

He laughed and tweaked her nose. "We'll find another way. Come on. I'll help you finish picking the letters off that shirt so you can put Laredo's name on it. At least we can count on *him*.''

Chapter Seven

Laredo stared at the beautiful woman in front of him. "Lied to me? Why?"

Cissy gave him a sweet smile. "All's fair in love and war. At least that's what I always heard. But now I don't think that's right anymore. I want to be on *your* side, Laredo."

He wasn't buying this act for a second. "Why?"

"I like you," she said, her tone innocent and shy.

Hmm. Still telling lies, but at least the kind he liked to hear. "Thought you liked my brother Ranger."

"I like him, too," she said earnestly.

Double hmm. "You just like men in general."

"You might say that." She curled a finger down the buttons of his shirt. "But I like you *best*."

This girl was a bad'un, and he wasn't in the mood for a reform fantasy. "Listen, this is serious, Cissy, for a lot of people. I can't play games with you. I have to beat your salon's bull, and I aim to do it."

She pursed her lips at him. "You need me on

your side, Laredo, giving you inside info, if you know what I mean.''

''You'd rat out your own salon?''

''If there was something in it for me,'' she said silkily.

Uh, yeah. Economics 101—there was no such thing as a free lunch. Laredo shrugged. ''What's the something?''

''A ride out of town.''

He stared at her. ''Bus, plane, train. They're all transporting, I hear. Especially trains, since this town is still a working station.''

''I'd rather someone I know take me where I want to go.''

There was a trap being laid here. Laredo just hadn't sprung it right. ''Where do you want to go?''

''Anywhere, as long as you're taking me.''

He stepped back from her shirt-roving hand. ''Cissy, I wouldn't dream of driving off with you. People would be looking for my body for months.''

She laughed. ''We're not *that* determined to win.''

''No, but you're working me for some reason. I suspect you're supposed to lure me out of town and then knock me out until the rodeo's over.''

''You're so suspicious!'' She smiled at him. ''Are you always like this?''

Since he'd met her? ''Yes.''

''Oh, piffle. You're just letting that crazy Katy Goodnight make you nuts.''

''Crazy?''

"Sure." She blinked at him. "Everybody knows she wouldn't let her ex-fiancé kiss her. So he dumped her. Big surprise, huh? I mean, virginity shouldn't be a remote-control trap, should it?"

Whoa! His mouth instantly dried out. "Virginity?"

"Well, if she won't let her fiancé kiss her, she sure wasn't going to get to normal relations."

"How do you know this?" He couldn't see Katy confiding in Cissy.

She laughed. "Laredo, this is a very small town. And we make it our business to know each other's business. Delilah and her girls act like unblemished southern ladies, but they keep tight tabs on us just like we do them." Cissy stepped between his legs so she could stare up at him with big eyes and a sultry mouth. "Depriving a man is cruel, Laredo. A man could lose his mind that way."

Wind blew through his brain in tunnel-like fashion. Cissy was standing too darn close to him. There was nothing remote-control about her trap. She was all about hands-on ambush. "Thanks for the tip on Bloodthirsty," he said, turning to head in the opposite direction. "If you'll excuse me, Miss Cissy, I've got to go."

If indeed Cissy was telling the truth this time, he had to tell his brothers. They had some major strategy revising to work on.

After that, he had to move out of Katy's room. A virgin? His tongue felt as if it had turned into a dry sponge. The first thought he'd ever had about Katy was that a man could spend many good nights with a girl like her!

He'd been way off the mark. No wonder he'd had trouble sleeping—he'd been in a virgin's bed. And he had two more nights to go!

He'd never make it. Sleep was going to be a thing of his past until he left Lonely Hearts Station, or until he vacated Katy's room. Every time he looked at Katy he thought about sex. Now, if he *could* get to sleep, he'd probably be dreaming about making love to her.

Being the first man in a woman's life was a load of responsibility.

It would also be a rush of major proportions. He'd never let that little gal out of his sight if he were her first....

That would not fit the doing-something-big plan.

Glancing up and down the street, he saw he had two choices for lodging: his truck and Miss Delilah's. As their champion, they felt it proper to put him up. He'd kissed Katy—and she'd virtually run away. Without sleep, he'd be mush by Saturday, and they'd have to pour him onto Bloodthirsty, and that bull would throw him to kingdom come. He'd wind up sleeping in a hospital.

Slowly he walked back into the Lonely Hearts Salon and climbed the stairs to Katy's room, where he knew he'd find her.

KATY TURNED as Laredo walked into her room. He looked different, worried. "What's wrong?"

Silent for a moment, he finally said, "I'm sorry I kissed you."

She only kept her lips from parting in surprised disappointment by the greatest effort. "Sorry?"

"I shouldn't have forced myself on you." Laredo rubbed his chin and then the back of his neck. "You were right to...reject my advance."

"Oh," she murmured. How much could words hurt a heart? Hannah said the heart was only a symbol, but it sure felt like her symbol was breaking. She'd been wishing she wasn't such a chicken when it came to Laredo; she'd been envying Cissy, who could throw herself at men with such confident ease.

Yet Laredo was sorry he'd kissed her. And Stanley hadn't liked to.

There *was* something wrong with her. It was some kind of weird spinsteritis. Men sensed it as soon as they touched her.

She had hoped it would be different with Laredo. She had hoped *she* would be different. "It's all right," she murmured. "Kissing's not that big a deal."

Of course, it was to her, but she wasn't going to make Laredo feel bad over her lack of sex appeal.

He looked surprised at her statement. "It's not?"

She shrugged. "Not really."

"Well...I'm surprised to hear you say that. You practically set a record running away from me."

A blush burned across her cheeks. "I was caught off guard."

"You said you weren't the girl for me. But I'm not looking for a girl for me."

She blinked. "What are you looking fŏr?"

"Adventure. And that's just about it."

Kissing with no strings attached. That certainly took all the pressure off. "I like to be adventurous."

He grinned at her, knowing at once that she was fibbing, she supposed. "Well, I'd like to be adventurous," she added.

"I don't have any plans tonight," he said.

"Are you asking me out?" After she'd run away from him like a scared rabbit, why would he?

"Friends can go out, can't they?"

"Friends?"

He nodded. "I promise not to kiss you again."

Her heart sank. "Okay," she said, trying to be a good sport.

"If that's what you want."

"Oh, yeah, yeah, sure. It's what I want." Well, not really, but she was in a bit deep here, and he was standing in her bedroom. Laredo didn't really stand, he lounged, or maybe it was *loomed,* because he towered over her. She'd never been alone with him like this, and never in such close proximity to a bed, and if they started kissing again like they had just a few hours ago, the virgin part of her might unfreeze and she'd jump him and then where would they be?

In bed.

She wasn't certain that would be such a bad thing. On the other hand, he'd just said he wouldn't kiss her again. That didn't sound like a man who could be jumped.

Strange. She'd never thought about jumping Stanley.

"What kind of friendly date did you have in mind?" she asked.

"Tell me what's in this town."

"Um, lots of unmarried women."

"One woman per date, I always say."

She rolled her eyes at him. "We could go riding."

"We could go for a walk and see what kind of trouble we could find," he suggested. "Seems there's always something brewing here."

"We could go lay pennies on the train track. The eight-thirty will come through tonight."

"Katy," he said suddenly, "what kind of dates have you been on lately?" He went around the fiancé issue, not wanting Katy to know that he had been filled in on her broken heart.

Or maybe not-so-broken heart. She didn't look all that broken-up to him.

She way-too-casually studied her fingernails. "Oh, you know, the usual."

He thought about that for a minute. "I haven't dated in a while. I'm rusty. What's the usual?"

"Mostly watching TV at my folks' house."

"I've got an idea," Laredo said. "Let's go for a drive."

"Where?"

"Nowhere. Out in the country, with some blankets and some beer. We'll lie in the truck bed and count the stars.''

Her eyes got round. "That almost sounds…romantic.''

No way was he going to let her get scared off again. If he knew anything about Katy Goodnight now, it was that she didn't know what a really good night was.

And he wasn't going to be the one to show her.

"Nah,'' he said, "it's the cheap man's entertainment. Beer and a truck bed for stargazing.''

"All right,'' Katy said. "We can drive down to the creek. Let me change into some jeans and grab my blanket. You get the beer.''

"Do you want to invite Hannah along?'' he asked, hoping she'd say no but wanting to make her more comfortable. It was so hard to be considerate when it was far more appealing to be alone with her!

"Oh,'' she said, her tone surprised.

Belatedly he realized he'd given her the wrong impression. "No, I mean that—''

But she'd already gone to the door. "Hannah!'' she called down the hall.

"What?'' Her friend poked her head around the doorway.

"Do you want to go for a drive with Laredo and me?''

"Sure!''

Katy looked at him. "She wants to come.''

"Great,'' he said. "Just great.''

IN LAREDO'S TRUCK Katy made certain Hannah sat between them. It had surprised her that Laredo had wanted Hannah along, but it made sense, along with his promise not to kiss her again.

She wasn't about to show how hurt she was. This was almost an instant replay of Stanley and Becky. She always seemed drawn to men who wanted her best friends, she thought. She was definitely sending off the wrong signals.

She had to get this problem figured out.

Surely she wasn't such a rotten kisser. If she was, she was looking at possibly being rotten in the love-making venue, as well—and that was a thought she could barely contemplate.

Maybe she had it all wrong! It wasn't celibacy she needed. It was practice! Practice made perfect, she'd always heard—and from this moment forward, she would resolve to practice with enthusiasm. In fact, she was going to throw all caution to the wind and become a Cissy Kisserton type of girl! "I've made up my mind," she told her two companions.

"What?" Laredo and Hannah said, both glancing her way as the truck bumped over tall weeds and rutted road to get to the side of the creek.

"I'm going to become free and uninhibited. A virtuoso mantrap."

Laredo swerved on the road. *"What?"*

Hannah stared at her. "Virtuoso? Aren't you already?"

"No," she said, with rolled eyeballs for Hannah's

benefit. "That's something else, which I aim not to be anymore."

Laredo perked up. "As your very good, extremely fond friend, I hereby put my services forward in *any* way I can to help you."

Katy blinked. "You don't even know what kind of help I need."

"Well, I…still resolve to help my very good friend," he said, looking past Hannah at Katy.

The light in his eyes had changed from I'm driving to I'm driving toward something, and Katy was suspicious. "Since when am I your very good friend?"

"Since we kissed and agreed we weren't going to do that anymore."

"You two kissed?" Hannah said.

"Not very well," Katy said.

"What?" Laredo looked outraged. "I didn't hear you complaining!"

"You kissed me, actually. I didn't kiss you back. And it was too short of a kiss to tell, really. Didn't you think?" Katy stated earnestly.

"Well, I don't know. I've never had a play-by-play called on my kissing skills." Laredo scratched his head. "Possibly you weren't engaged in the moment. But I can work on that, as I help you achieve mantrap status."

"I don't need a coach," she snapped.

"No, no, no. I see myself more as a *partner*."

"Why are you so anxious for our Katy to become a mantrap?" Hannah asked.

"I was wondering the same thing." Katy gave him a suspicious glare. "You know, don't you?"

"That you're...you're...special?" Laredo said, carefully choosing his words. "That you're a discriminating female?"

"That I'm a virgin," Katy said flatly. "Who told you?"

"If I tell you, it's a breach of confidence," he said, sidestepping.

"Hannah?" Katy stared at her friend.

"Not me." Hannah raised her hands. "I only advise from the sidelines. I don't coach from the middle of the field."

"Who?" both women demanded, turning to stare at Laredo.

"Cissy Kisserton," he said, his face pinkening a bit.

"Cissy! How does she know?" Katy demanded.

"She says everybody in town knows." Laredo cleared his throat. "It's not a CIA-encoded secret, apparently."

Katy leaned back against the headrest. "I see. And so now you're offering to help me achieve my goals because..."

"Because he wants to go where no man has gone before," Hannah intoned.

"I'm just being a good friend," Laredo insisted.

"Shut up," both women said.

"What was in it for Cissy Kisserton? Why did she tell you this?" Katy asked. "Just so I can understand why she was discussing my personal business. This couldn't have had anything to do with riding our bull this weekend.''

''I think it did,'' Laredo said, confused. ''Actually, I can't remember how we got onto the subject. Something about you driving men crazy because you deprived them.''

''What?''

''Yep. That's what she said,'' Laredo said with satisfaction. ''You had an ex-fiancé who took exception to your, um—''

''Okay. I've heard enough. Take me home,'' Katy demanded. ''At once.''

''Hey, I didn't ask her to tell me any of this. And trust me, I left as soon as I realized nothing good was going to come of the conversation. She just wanted me to know that she'd lied about Bloodthirsty Black's crank out of the chute, and the chatter went downhill from there.''

Katy glared at him. ''Is that why you asked me out tonight on a poor man's date? Isn't that what you called it?''

''No. I like driving around. I like hanging out. Frankly, you're not the kind of friend I feel I have to take to a hundred-dollar restaurant to make happy, since we agreed that you're not the right woman for me, and I don't want a woman, anyway. But I will take you to a hundred-dollar restaurant, if you'd prefer that. It's just, then we won't be friends, we'll be nuts.''

She sat back again. ''One of these days, Cissy is

going to open her mouth too wide and find herself in big trouble.''

''I couldn't agree more,'' Laredo said cheerfully. ''But I don't think you should become a mantrap unless you allow me to be the one to spring your hinge. Practice on me, Katy.''

She looked back at him. Hannah giggled. ''It is so weird being in the middle of this conversation. Katy wants practice, Laredo wants to give it to her, and I'm tagging along as mediator, I think.''

''Thank heaven,'' Katy said.

''Yeah,'' Laredo agreed, ''because I don't think I would have been brave enough to bring this up without a witness to my good intentions. We haven't gotten along very well up to this point. Have you noticed that?''

''It's pent-up sexual attraction,'' Hannah said with a nod. ''We should have brought your brothers. At least then we could have double-dated. Or would that be a triple date?''

''This is not a date,'' Laredo and Katy said at the same time.

''It's not if the definition of *date* is individuals engaging in simultaneously pleasing activity, but whatever,'' Hannah said. ''Let's play strip poker at the creek edge.''

Katy stared at her. ''Strip poker.''

''It's my favorite game,'' Hannah said, pulling cards out of her duffel-shaped purse. ''Remember, I told you that.''

Laredo put the truck into gear and rolled forward

a few hundred feet to park beside the creek. "It's gotta be my favorite game, too, but only when I win. And when I'm with beautiful women." He gave a mock leer at Hannah and Katy. "I should warn you, I cheat."

"We know," Katy said. "It shows in the company you've been keeping."

"Actually, I don't admire Cissy at all for lying to me. Even though she was trying to undo what she'd done," Laredo said self-righteously.

"I think there's a difference between cheating and lying," Hannah said. "Cheating can be honorable if the game rules allow for it. Then it's creative competition. But a lie is just smarmy."

"That's it," Laredo agreed. "Cissy must have been covering something up, or she wouldn't have come clean about the lie. She's working on two tiers, is what I think."

"What else could she be doing?" Katy asked.

"Trying to throw me off track. Exactly what was it they did with the last cowboy?"

Hannah shuffled the card deck on her knees. "They lured him."

"Okay. I'm not the kind of guy who can be lured."

Both women stared at him incredulously. Then Katy shrugged, opening the truck door. "Come on. Let's spread out in the truck bed where we can think this through better."

"A beer will definitely help my thinking process," Laredo agreed cheerfully. He pulled down the truck gate and they piled in, each grabbing a blanket to sit on. They pulled beers from the cooler, and then the cooler became a table for the cards.

"This night sky is gorgeous," Hannah said. "And that will help *my* thinking process. Don't take your shoes off, Katy. You need them for the game."

"No, no," Laredo disagreed. "Remember, she wants the practice of being a mantrap. I'm willing to let her practice on me, and she can start by being near naked."

"That's assuming you win," Katy said frostily, "and I don't intend for that to happen. You eliminated yourself from practicing with me when you discussed me with Cissy."

"Picky, picky," he said. "Take your shoes off if you want."

"I'll keep them on. All night, more than likely." She gave him a level stare, but Laredo grinned at her.

"All right, back to the plan," Hannah said, dealing hands. "You're not the kind of guy who can be lured, you say. But sex is their great weapon, and hey, we all know a guy can't pass that up."

Laredo cleared his throat as Katy's gaze stayed on him. "Well, it is a lot to ask, but sacrifices are necessary at times. And the Lonely Hearts ladies did a lot for my family last month. I can refuse luring."

Hannah put down one card, while Laredo and Katy asked for three.

"If you're the dealer, aren't you supposed to go last?" Laredo asked.

"This is just a friendly game of poker," Hannah said. "Just something to help me concentrate." They all turned up their cards, drawing a smirk from Hannah. "Choose your article of clothing, cowboy."

Good-naturedly, he pulled off a boot and tossed it over the edge of the truck. "Opening-round bad luck."

Katy raised her brows. "If Laredo continues to resist Cissy, they'll try another tack."

"Right." Hannah nodded as she dealt another hand. "And you've got the *if* handled?"

Laredo nodded. "The *if* is not even a problem. I'm pretty certain that sex with Cissy would be one of those trips into the phantasmagoric wonderland of excess a man tries diligently to avoid."

The women stared at him.

"Right," Hannah said, her brows raised. "Then we have to be prepared for sabotage, I suppose."

"Sabotage!" Katy dropped another three cards. "You don't mean our bull?"

"It's possible," Hannah said. "It's either our stud or our bull. That's sort of how Marvella thinks."

"Hey!" Laredo exclaimed.

"Her steely mind adds up our weapons. But I still think Marvella would never believe that Cissy couldn't pull off enticing Laredo," Hannah continued blithely.

He finished a beer and tossed the empty into the cooler. "You girls make it sound like I'm so easy," he complained, grabbing another beer. "I'm not like other guys."

They turned over their cards.

"I lost again," Laredo said, disbelieving. "Are you cheating, Katy?"

"Me?" She shook her head. "But speaking of cheating, who is the Never Lonely Cut-N-Gurls cowboy? Does anybody know?"

"That might help us, if we knew that in advance," Hannah said.

"Would you steal him?" Laredo asked. "Isn't that a lying, cheating combination? *And* copying the enemy's game plan?"

"Shh," Hannah told him. "I'm going to call Cissy and ask, since she's such a blabbermouth these days." Pulling out a cell phone, she punched in some numbers. "Of course, she's probably busy on a Thursday night," she said snidely. "Laredo, don't forget to remove an article of clothing. Hello, Cissy? Hannah. Sitting here playing strip poker with Laredo and Katy. Yes, I am. Laredo's losing. He's down two boots." She held up the phone. "Say 'hello, Cissy,' you guys."

Laredo and Katy dutifully called, "Hello, Cissy."

"So, Cissy, we were wondering, what cowboy do you have riding Bad-Ass Blue this weekend? I was talking to the copywriter for the *Lonely Hearts Station Dispatch* today, and I couldn't remember for the life of me who you'd told me it was. And they want it for their article, you know," she said, holding up two crossed fingers to show that she was fibbing through her teeth.

She listened for a few moments. "Oh, I see. Okay. Well, good luck. Bye." Turning off the phone, she stared at Laredo for a moment. "They don't have a rider yet," she said, amazed. "That's the second tier."

"What is?" Laredo and Katy asked in unison.

"You. That's why Marvella pulled out all the stops and sicced Cissy on you. Marvella's obviously hoping Cissy can change your mind so that you'll be *their* rider instead."

Katy gasped. "They wouldn't stoop that low!"

"Why else would Cissy make certain Laredo knew about your...um, lack of experience?" she said tactfully.

Katy and Laredo stared at each other. "To make me look bad," Katy said. "Not as worldly and sophisticated."

"She was saying, Here's something and over there you get nothing. So ride our bull, because there's benefits to it you never even dreamed of."

"Okay." Laredo sat up straight. "Listen to me carefully. I'm going to ride Bloodthirsty Black this weekend, and then I'm leaving town."

Katy looked at him. "If he leaves now, then neither of us has a rider."

"I'm not leaving," Laredo said. "Are you saying you think I should leave?"

"No, but if they think you're gone, maybe they'll settle down," Katy pointed out.

"You're kind of crafty," Laredo said with admiration. "I don't think you've shown me this side of you yet."

Katy gave him an arch look. "I haven't shown you any sides of me."

"They've got to find somebody by Saturday morning." Hannah put the cards down. "They have one day."

"I don't know," Laredo said. "Maybe Cissy was lying again."

"And that could be, too," Hannah said. "Okay, it's hot, and I vote we swim. Then we'll think some more."

"Swim in what?" Katy asked doubtfully.

"Anything you want to." Hannah hopped out of the truck. "Last one in the creek is a cow patty!" She pulled off her top and sprinted a few yards away from the truck. Katy and Laredo followed, peeling clothes as they ran.

"Whee!" Katy yelled, feeling free and uninhibited and fun for the first time in a long time. In white cotton bra and panties, she jumped into the creek, hearing the giant splash Laredo made behind her. They sprayed water at each other madly for a couple of seconds, and then the sound of a truck engine halted their horseplay.

"See ya!" Hannah called from the truck, joyfully waving Laredo's jeans out the window. "I left you a blanket over there, and the cooler. Be back in a few hours, kids!"

And then she drove off.

Leaving Katy alone in a creek with Laredo, and neither of them wearing more than underwear. At least, she hoped Laredo had underwear on…she glanced nervously toward the water's edge, but she didn't see anything that looked like underwear on the bank.

Hopefully he still had it on, she thought, gazing at his hard chest and muscular shoulders.

And that dark intense look was back in his eyes as he stared at her chest the same way she'd stared at his. Then his gaze met hers, pinning her, it felt, with heat.

"Practice makes perfect, Katy Goodnight," Laredo said. "I think we should start your lessons tonight."

Then he put his arms around her, drawing her against him.

She glanced up at him. "Laredo, maybe I haven't decided that you're the most credible teacher for me."

Chapter Eight

"Why not?" Laredo demanded, surprised that Katy would sound so indifferent to him. He certainly was not indifferent to her. In fact, he was afraid that despite the cold water, he might do serious injury to himself by bursting a muscle somewhere in his groin area if she didn't hurry up and say yes.

At this moment, her tone was more truculent than he liked. *Truculent* was a word he'd never heard anyone use except on a *Peanuts* cartoon he'd watched once when his brothers were younger, but at this moment, staring down into Katy's blazing eyes and soft, pouty mouth, he knew he was looking at truculence personified.

"You're too cocky," she said. "Which is good in a bull rider, but not in a kiss mate."

"Cocky," he repeated. "I am who I am."

"Yes," she said on a sigh, "I realize that. While I can accept it, that doesn't mean I have to like it."

"Katy," he said in some desperation, "a kiss isn't forever. I swear my lips aren't cocky. If you just stand still a moment, I can clear up all your doubts about your kissing skills.''

She shrugged enticingly bare shoulders at him, rounded skin that gleamed above the dark water and hinted at the sweetness bobbing just beneath.

How he wished it was daylight so he could see her better!

''A kiss could be forever,'' she insisted. ''If it's done right. Not like that little peck we shared yesterday. You're already telling me you're not going to do it right this time. And why should I participate in that?''

''Katy, no one kisses for forever.''

''But that's my problem, Laredo,'' she said. ''Stanley didn't kiss me with his whole heart. Although Hannah says that the heart is not really involved, that it's basically an allegorical muscle, I don't buy that.''

''What?'' Laredo had serious heat beneath the waist, and she was trying to fry his brain with deep thoughts. ''Hey, I just want to taste you, Katy Goodnight. You know, between friends.''

''Nope.'' She kicked toward the shore and got out, streaming water down her long ponytail, running droplets down her back, into her panties, which showed a wonderful delineation of well-rounded bottom—

''There's no such thing as a real kiss between friends,'' Katy called over her shoulder.

''Wait, wait, wait. You're going about this all wrong.'' He got out of the water, walked up the bank, picked Katy up and strode back into the water with her.

"Laredo—"

"You said we'd think better when we were wet, and I'm certain this water is easing my thought passages. Like soda bubbles need syrupy water to get through a straw. Now, listen, Katy, you're going about this mantrap business all wrong. I offered to let you practice on me. You're supposed to use me and abuse me."

"I am?" Her glare turned to question.

"Oh, absolutely. Most definitely. Take advantage of me. Lay your lips on me and then say goodbye. Kiss and flee, leaving me crying."

"Oh, I wouldn't want to hurt your feelings—"

"Katy, I swear, I won't cry in front of you. Now, pucker up. Please."

She cocked a brow at him. "Stanley never said *that* to me."

He squinted his eyes at her. "Stanley clearly didn't know all the magic words. I'm going to teach you how to be the best mantrap in town. Manmagnet of the century. Cissy Kisserton won't be able to touch your talent. You practice on me, and we'll both get so good, we'll open up a kissing booth at the next rodeo. We'll make a fortune for charity."

She wound her arms around his neck, and he looked down, enjoying the view of flat tummy and puckered nipples through a cotton bra sticking to all the things he wanted it stuck to.

"Okay, Laredo," she said softly. "Let's practice."

Thank heaven. Yee-haw! All his smooth talking had gotten him just what he wanted. He was going to kiss this little girl; he was going to dazzle her until there were stars in her eyes she couldn't shake out....

Holding her closer, he placed his lips against hers, making certain he gentled her, like a rider with a new mare.

To his surprise Katy locked her lips onto his, sucking and pulling, and then changing pressure as she moved her lips to a different position. Her breasts snuggled up against his chest as her hands clasped the back of his head. Her lips and tongue did a sex dance all over his mouth. The heat in his groin exploded into a raging fire.

Suddenly she pulled away and stared up at him with big, blue innocent eyes. "Was that right?"

His legs were trembling from the afterburn. "Uh, yeah," he said, "I think we've got something to work with."

"HEY!" Hannah called, interrupting Tex and Ranger as they stood eyeing Bloodthirsty Black. The brothers turned around, and she tossed Laredo's truck keys at them.

Ranger caught them with a deft hand. "You look like a windblown daisy. What have you been doing?"

"Playing strip poker with your brother and Katy."

Tex stared at her. "If you're here, does that mean you won?"

"It means I think quicker than them. It's hard to get those two to cut to the chase. They just dance around the whole issue like Baryshnikov's ballet—"

"What issue?" Ranger demanded.

"Sex," Hannah said. "Love. Rock 'n' roll. You know."

Ranger stared at her, somewhat bemused. "Are they having sex? Or rocking 'n' rolling?"

"I doubt they're doing either. Or anything other than swimming. Last I saw them, they were nearly naked in Barmaid's Creek, which for most people would be encouraging." She sighed heavily. "But not for Katy and Laredo. They're probably still arguing about who's going to make the first move tonight. Or ever, for that matter."

"My brother's pretty slow on the uptake," Ranger said.

"And Katy's too smart for her own good. Can do bio, organic, almost any kind of chemistry you care to name, but she has no sense when it comes to the sexual kind."

"I don't care to try to name any of them," Ranger said. "Although organic sounds like it'd be right up Tex's alley."

"Not right now," Tex said. "I'm focused on Malicious Bull Riding 101."

"So you left them in the creek?" Ranger asked.

Hannah nodded. "Do you mind fishing them out in a couple of hours? They'll be too mad at me, and I'm afraid they'll take their revenge by sending me down the creek-fall in nothing but my bra and underwear."

"Sounds vengeful but inviting," Ranger said on a rough breath. "Maybe you should accompany me to pick up the lovebirds."

"Oh, make no mistake about it," Hannah said with a patient expression, "they are far from lovebirds. They'll peck each other's feathers out before they admit that they might like each other."

"It's a Jefferson curse," Tex said on a long-suffering sigh. "We never settle down, and then when we do—"

"When we do?" Ranger interrupted. "The only one who has is Frisco, and he was a freak case."

"Why?" Hannah asked.

"Oh, it was that storm or something. All that rain diluted his brain." Ranger turned his attention to the bull in the stall. "It all went south when he broke his leg, in my estimation."

"Yeah, Helga trapped him, and he darn near went mad with the daily emotional trauma of her caring for him. So he was ripe for the picking. But as you can tell, Laredo is in fine physical and emotional shape," Tex said. "He may not be very sua-vay at dating, but he's definitely on target to avoid falling in love."

Hannah stared at the two of them. "You're both full of wind, but I suppose you're harmless enough.

Please don't forget to pick your brother and Katy up in a bit." And she walked away.

"Hey! Don't leave," Ranger called. "You should ride out to the creek with us."

She waved and kept on walking. A few more strides and she disappeared.

"That's one crazy lil' ol' gal," Ranger said with wonder. "Leaving my brother in nothing but his Calvins in a creek somewhere."

"That sounds like a Mimi trick," Tex said, his tone just as impressed. "And we thought only Mimi had that type of superspunk."

"Good thing we're not interested in a woman at this time," Ranger said, his gaze turning to his brother.

"Yeah, man. Let's get back to this bull," Tex agreed. "He has just a little less crank to him than Hannah."

"True," Ranger murmured, his gaze bouncing back to the exit Hannah had used. "Just a little less crank. But a helluva liftoff."

"WHAT I WANT TO KNOW," Laredo said, as he placed a beer bottle cap on his bare stomach to show Katy that he could roll just as well as she could, "is why you agreed to marry that Stanley guy in the first place. If he didn't like to kiss you, that is. Isn't sucking face a basic building block for a successful marriage?"

Katy lay very still on her back on the blanket Laredo had laid down for them. She focused her stomach muscles to move slowly, so that the beer cap on her belly made a guided flip, flip, flip motion up her stomach. "I fell in love with Stanley, not with his sexual prowess."

Laredo grimaced. "I guess not."

"Did you ever fall in love with anyone?" Katy asked, taking the beer cap off her stomach and re-settling it lower.

The question interrupted his successful rolling of the beer cap. "I was up to two rolls until you asked me that," he charged. "You should never ask a man about love when he's trying to align his stomach muscles into the perfect gyration for beer cap rolling."

She put two beer caps on her stomach and began crunching her muscles so that the two caps moved upward in unison. Laredo sighed and sat up. "I'm not going to be able to beat you at this game. How about we try one of mine?"

"Answer the question," she told Laredo, putting a third cap on her stomach.

"No. I've never had a hankering to fall in love."

She frowned. "One doesn't always get a hankering. Sometimes love just hits."

"Did you have a hankering? Or a hit?"

"A hankering. Actually, I'd studied so long to be good at my chosen profession that I think I really wanted a fling. The kind the other girls had when they went on spring break."

"Katy," Laredo said, "when your friends went to the beach for spring break, they were not going to find a husband. Subconsciously you picked stability.''

''I know. Well, marrying Stanley felt as wild and crazy as I could be. However, after living around Hannah for a while, I've decided to change. I'm going to up my footloose meter.''

''Excellent. Can I make a swimsuit top for you out of beer caps?'' Laredo asked.

She stopped rolling her stomach, which made him feel slightly less hypnotized. On the other hand, if she could move her muscles that well, imagine what other muscles she could utilize—

''Laredo, I said, go ahead.''

''Oh.'' His mouth watered as she accepted his invitation. Of course, he hadn't been serious. He'd been teasing, certain of a *No!* ''Well, to make a proper swim top,'' he said, trying to sound knowledgeable, ''you'd have to take off the one you're currently wearing.''

She sat up, turning her back to him.

''What?'' he asked dumbly.

''Unhook me.''

His fingers started gently trembling. Maybe he'd drunk too much beer. That was it! He didn't have enough caps for a proper beer-cap top. He counted three Katy had rolled on her stomach, and two on the ground beside him. There was an old one someone had tossed away; he could use that one. It would be an even number, he thought, his mind hazy with rapid-fire counting. He could cover her decently with six caps. One each for her nipples, which left four caps, two per breast...

He was going to lose his mind in the process.

"Laredo," Katy said, turning her head to glance at him, "maybe you are all bull and no consummation."

"Ahem." He cleared his throat, reaching a tentative hand toward her back.

But then he pulled his hand away. If Katy thought kissing was forever, then making love to her would be lifetimes into infinity. If not infinity, at least into googolplex, a word he thought Miss Smarty Pants might be impressed that he knew.

"A googol is ten to the hundredth power; a googolplex is ten to the googol power," he said, wishing desperately he was brave enough to accept her invitation. The thought of seeing her bare breasts was enough to scissor his brain in two. "A googolplex is the largest named number. Bet you didn't think I knew that."

Her eyes widened. "Do you always delve into mathematical jargon when you're undecided?"

"I was trying to get my mind off my hormones. It's not working."

She let her gaze roam downward. "So I see."

Taking a deep breath, he said, "Katy, I think I'll rescind my creative offer of a beer cap top."

"Because?"

"Because I won't be able to stop there. I'll want to make you a beer cap thong—"

"And then we'll be drunk..."

"And then we'll be drunk, and then…then I might make love to you but neither of us would remember it, and your first time should be special," he said on a rush, happy to have found reasoning that sounded sane.

"I want to," Katy said softly. "I want you to be the first."

"Why me?" Laredo had never heard such sweet words, but he truly was not the man to act upon them.

"Because you're sexy. And macho. And I'm going to Duke after the summer, and I'll probably fall for another of my own kind—"

"Your own kind?"

"Some studious, boring, tenure-bound professor, and I'll have missed the opportunity to have a hot cowboy take my virginity. That sounds like a woman's dream fantasy come true, don't you think?"

He wasn't sure about a woman, but he knew the fantasy sure as hell had him standing straight up. "Katy," he rasped, "you've got to quit talking like that. I can only take so much."

"Uh-uh," she said, turning all the way around and situating herself between his legs so that she faced him, "This is the new me. Remember?"

"I like the old you," he said desperately.

"Yes, but the old me lived in her fears. She was a shell without adventure or fearlessness. I don't want to be a chem prof with no sinful side explored."

"The right man is out there," Laredo said, hanging on to no with all his might. "The one who'll stay around and give you children and a secure house and a solid marriage. The one who'll take you to church on Sunday and give you an iron for Mother's Day and—"

"Laredo, you're more afraid of making love to me than riding Bloodthirsty Black," Katy murmured against his neck.

Goose pimples exploded on his body. "Fear is a healthy emotion."

"It kicks the fight-or-flight mechanism into gear," she whispered into his ear, before nibbling on it.

"I'm flighting," he said.

"I think you're the right man for my adventure," Katy said. "Of course, if you don't want to—"

It was all a man could bear. It was endurance beyond expectation. He rolled Katy onto her back, pinning her beneath him. "Katy Goodnight," he said, "you have driven me past no."

She actually laughed at him. "Good. I'm working on that vixen side of my personality."

He tore her little cotton bra straps down with his teeth, until he revealed each breast. "Oh my God," he murmured. "You are perfect."

A door slammed somewhere up the bank. "Hey, Laredo!" Ranger called. A loud, annoying moose mating call erupted from Ranger as his footsteps seemed to head their way.

"Are you down there, bro?" Tex yelled, his voice

cutting through the darkness. "Your rescue crew has arrived and is reporting for duty!"

Katy stared up at Laredo with huge eyes. By the moon's light, Laredo could see her hard nipples topping sweetly rounded breasts only inches from his mouth. "I'm going to *kill* my brothers," he growled. "The biblical Cain had *nothing* on me."

Chapter Nine

It was a very quiet ride back. Laredo had dropped the blanket over her shoulders to protect her body from his brothers' inquiring gazes. They were trying to be gentlemen, but of course, they were curious as to why she only wore a blanket. Not that they verbalized the question, but the expressions on their faces were priceless.

"Uh, Hannah didn't say anything about you not having clothes," Tex said.

"I'm sure she didn't," Laredo bit out. "Come on, Katy." He helped her into the back of the extended cab, covering her with an extra blanket from the truck bed.

Katy's hair was wild and matted from swimming, and her heart was disappointed. She'd been so close to being a femme fatale. Or at least an unmade maiden.

"That was it?" Hannah demanded once Katy made it into her room.

"That was it. We didn't even say a proper goodnight, because Tex and Ranger dragged him off with them." Katy was totally dejected.

"All my planning for nothing. I really thought I'd worked it to where you two had no reason not to manage the miraculous."

Katy crawled into bed beside Hannah. "Apparently not. He was babbling about googolplexes at one point, so I'm pretty certain he was relieved when the cavalry arrived."

"He'll be asleep in your room tonight. Just crawl in bed beside him. Maybe even on top of him. Trust me, he won't kick you out."

Katy sighed. "Yeah, but I've had time to think about it. Laredo's right. We shouldn't do it."

"Because?" Hannah's voice was incredulous in the darkness.

"He doesn't really want to. I mean, the body is willing but the spirit is very reluctant."

"You could change his mind if you wanted to."

Katy thought about that and then closed her eyes. As easygoing, available, macho as he'd tried to make himself sound, she'd figured one thing out: Laredo wasn't a man to womanize. He didn't fall in love easily or willingly. And she couldn't just take advantage of him as he'd suggested.

He *was all* bull and no consummation.

Bull rider, in this case. And nothing more than that.

RANGER AND LAREDO SAT in the Lonely Hearts Cafeteria, stewing. "You'd better be careful," Ranger said. "I think that bull is gonna whap you upside the head, 'cause you're not thinking straight."

It was true. Laredo's mind was still in a twist over Katy in a wet bra and pair of panties. It had taken all his strength to keep her pure, and he'd just about not made it. "I'm in no condition to ride a bull," he admitted. "Specifically since I don't know how."

"Well, the competition doesn't know that." Ranger forked some steak and chewed.

"The competition doesn't even have a cowboy riding yet."

Ranger brightened, then his face fell. "No, a forfeit is too much to hope for."

"Besides, I should ride. I owe it to myself to ride," Laredo said. "It's my first Big Thing on my list of Big Things To Do."

"And after this? Then what?"

"Then I'm continuing on my trek. Searching out opportunity and adventure." He thought about Katy for a second. There was opportunity and adventure in abundance, but not really the kind a man could boast about. Not like riding a bull, or collecting yak hair in the Andes. "Are there yaks in the Andes?" Laredo asked.

His brother stared at him. "You dope. Do I look like a reference point for Yaks-R-Us? How the hell would I know?"

"I don't know." Laredo scratched at his neck. "I just always had the idea that our family was smart. Above average, intellectually."

Ranger put down his fork. "We work, and we do

all right. We've all got some talent at something. We drink too much beer, and sometimes we let women chase us around town. That's above average, I'd say.''

Not enough to measure up to a whiz like Katy, though. "Remember Joey Forrester?''

"The science geek you rolled up in a carpet and set on top of Mrs. Fisk's desk? You called him the human enchilada for your science project. What was the theme again, anyway?''

Laredo rolled his eyes. "Something about digestion. I can't remember now. Do you know what happened to Joey?''

"Yeah. He married some science geekess and they gave birth to lots of Einsteinian tots. He teaches at Harvard, and she teaches at the equivalent, while breastfeeding on the three-year plan while she crusades for women's issues. I think they're both up for some kind of academic recognition.'' Ranger ate a roll with butter on it. "Boy, they sure know how to cook in this town. And it is a change from Helga and her sauerkraut. I may never go home, either. I have been thinking about joining the military, you know.''

Laredo nodded, not really hearing his brother's kibitzing. That was exactly the future he could see for Katy: she'd marry some really smart guy, and they'd have extremely Mensa-qualified ankle biters who had their own Kappa keys given to them at birth by the latest Nobel Peace Prize winners.

"Yeah," he said, "But Helga's sauerkraut is home."

"You're not homesick yet, are you? You haven't even left the state."

"I know," Laredo said miserably. And when he did finally get out of the state, he had a funny feeling it wasn't going to be the sauerkraut he missed.

It would be Katy.

CISSY SMILED as she crept into the barn, stealthily moving up on the lone cowboy staring at the bull. Hannah had lied! And Cissy had been too quick to fall for that bait. Of course Laredo wasn't playing strip poker with Hannah and Katy. Like Katy would ever let her hair down, anyway. Strip poker?

Oh, Laredo had been around…but he hadn't been with Katy.

And now Cissy had her chance at having him alone, with no prying eyes anywhere around.

"Hi," she said softly.

He turned around, settling his hat back from his forehead. A big smile grew on his face. See! She'd known Laredo hadn't been immune to her. He'd just been too gentlemanly to put the moves on her.

Fine. She could play candy and cream just as well as Katy G. "Got that bull figured out?" she asked, standing next to him.

He stared down at her with eyes that didn't miss a thing, not her low-cut, waist-tied top, nor her long and shapely legs. Nor, by the appreciative sniff he gave her hair, her perfume.

"I don't know about the bull," Laredo told her, his eyes gleaming, "but maybe I'd rather figure you out."

"I promise, I'm a-b-c simple," she cooed.

He laughed and picked her up off her feet, settling her onto his waist. "I'm sure you are, darling. I'm sure you are."

Whew! He was more man than she'd bargained for. If she wasn't careful, Laredo was going to make her forget all her sugar-and-spice planning.

Before she realized what he was about, he was planting kisses in the opening of her blouse, between her breasts. She shivered, loving every second of it.

He popped the snap on her jean shorts and kissed her belly. She writhed, feeling herself come alive in a way she hadn't in a long time. Not for any man who'd come the Never Lonely Cut-N-Gurls' way.

Then he kissed above her knee, sliding his tongue along her inner thigh to the edge of her frayed shorts. Cissy tried to hold in a moan and wrapped her fingers in his hair, her mind swimming.

"How do you feel about hay?" he asked her.

She didn't care if the bed was made of rock salt. "Fine," she said on a gasp. "Just hurry."

Laredo grinned at her and carried her into a freshly filled stall. Tossing a clean blanket onto the ground, he lowered her to the floor.

This time, Cissy thought, the conquest was going to be so worth the chase.

AN HOUR LATER Cissy's knees were shaking and her body was melted sunshine. "You're a cutie," Laredo said against her breasts. "I could spend all night with you."

"Why don't you?" she asked, her body heating up again. "I've got a real soft bed."

He grinned. "Why don't I just? Show it to me, cutie."

Marvella was going to be so proud of her! Once he was inside the Never Lonely Cut-N-Gurls Salon, he was theirs for the keeping.

He would be her love slave.

He would be her bull rider. He wouldn't be able to say no to her feminine wiles.

Silently she took his hand and led him home. When she opened the door, all the girls who were sitting around the main area quieted.

"Good night, everyone," was all Cissy said, unwilling to share her catch. These girls were tricky, and she didn't dare let go of her prize for an instant.

Hurriedly, she pretty much dragged Laredo up the stairs and into her room. "Make yourself comfortable," she said.

"I plan to," he said, tackling her on the bed so that he landed beside her. Then he caught her lips in a lingering kiss that stole her breath.

When she could speak again, Cissy stared up at her lover. "I have to admit, I didn't think you had this much potential." Any man who was interested in Katy Goodnight had to have cold little pebbles for a brain!

He laughed at her. "You never know about a person, do you? It's us quiet ones that have all the attitude.'' Sliding her on top of him, still fully dressed, he situated her on his stomach. "You are a pretty little thing. When I go back home, I'm going to send you a week's worth of roses.''

She smiled. "Actually, I have something else in mind you can give me.''

RANGER AND LAREDO LEFT the Lonely Hearts Station Cafeteria. Ranger squinted up at the lights on the top floor of the Never Lonely Cut-N-Gurls Salon as they went out.

"So, what's up with that place, anyway?''

Laredo shrugged. "Don't know. Have no interest in finding out. Anyway, you were in there. What did you think?''

"That Cissy Kisserton is a wonderful kisser.''

"Are you interested in her?''

"Nah. No more than she was in me.''

Laredo eyed his brother. "Now, see, Katy isn't like that. She just isn't the type of girl to understand that a kiss can be just a kiss and nothing more.''

"You're not that kind of guy, either. Get over it.''

They walked past the Lonely Hearts Salon. Laredo sent a longing glance toward it. "I'd bet Katy's in bed by now.''

"Tuckered out after a long swim.'' Ranger chuckled. "Bet you wish you were in there with her, but it wouldn't do any damn good. Sort of the sexual *Twilight Zone,* complete with the do-do-do-do, do-

do-do-do background music. Scary, and with a twisted ending every time.''

''Shut up.'' Laredo didn't feel like being teased about Katy, or their swim, or their nonlovemaking potential.

''Hey, no problemo.'' Inside the barn they went to Bloodthirsty Black's pen, which was empty. ''Out to pasture, I guess. Nightly roam.''

''Wonder where Tex is?'' Laredo asked.

''Probably got tired of waiting for us and decided to bunk in for the night.''

Laredo nodded, not too worried about his twin. ''Guess I'll hit the sack myself.''

Ranger grinned. ''You do that. I'm not ready to turn in yet.''

''All right. Good night.'' Actually, he was glad to leave Ranger and head back to the salon. Maybe, if he was lucky, he'd get to see Katy.

But the salon and the halls were dark. There were some cookies on the kitchen counter with a note with his name on it, written by Miss Delilah.

He carried the cookies upstairs to his dark, empty room. Switching on the lamp beside his bed, he stared down at Rose the mouse. ''Miss me?''

She twitched her whiskers at him and ran into her tube.

''I'm the reserved type, too,'' he said.

The door closed. He turned, his brow raised, and Katy floated over to the bed in a long, slinky gown that looked like something a movie star would wear to bed.

"I thought I'd tuck you in," she said.

"Good idea," he said.

"That would be crossing the bounds of our friendship."

He was salivating for more than the cookies. "Yes, it would."

"And I wouldn't want to sap your strength before your bull ride."

"That's day after tomorrow. I recover quickly." She looked so pretty in the long white gown. Pink ribbons were tied around the neckline, and he itched to undo them with his teeth.

"I had a good time swimming with you, Laredo," she said. "I just want you to know that."

"I still owe you a beer cap bikini top." He could see her nipples through the satiny fabric. "One day I'll make you one."

"Good night," she said.

It was all friendly banter with no twist. Ranger was wrong. There was no background music; there was no *Twilight Zone* where they fell into an alternate reality and made love. Katy wasn't going to get in his bed. He really couldn't blame her, not after he'd given her the speech on not getting tied down. And he wasn't going to get into hers, not with the virgin reality hanging on his conscience.

Whoa, boy.

She looked at him, and he looked at her, and they both became uncomfortable. Then she was gone, and he was alone with Rose. The mouse didn't seem all that interested in him.

Stuffing the cookies in a napkin, he decided to eat them while he took a long walk to get rid of the sudden surge of energy running through his body.

"Back so soon?" Hannah asked.

"Scoot over." Katy slid into bed, completely dejected. "We're both all bull and no consummation. I couldn't get my nerve up to whisper anything seductive. It was pretty obvious he'd changed his mind."

"He was probably too shocked that you were in his room to grab you and divest you of your gown. Give him time to get used to the idea."

They heard the door down the hall open and close. A few seconds later they heard boots on the stairwell. Then the front door shut. Both girls flew to the window and peered out, to see Laredo walking down the street.

Katy sank back into the bed. "He probably thinks I'm chasing him. That is not a man who is dying to get me into his bed."

Hannah pulled the covers up to her chin. "You know, the right guy is probably waiting at Duke for you."

Katy tried to be happy about that, but the problem was, she couldn't be. It would be so bad to fall for a man who didn't like her, especially after her disastrous nonmarriage. "Do you think he's going to the enemy camp?"

"Nope."

Of course, that was where men went when they

needed to get some…peace of mind. Still, Laredo had told her he wasn't interested in Cissy. She believed him.

And yet…

"Is it wrong to follow a man?" she asked Hannah. "Does that fall under the heading of spying? Stalking? Prying?"

Hannah jumped from the bed. "I wasn't going to suggest it, but since you mentioned it, I think late-evening walks under any heading are healthier than lying awake. Hurry and get dressed!"

Chapter Ten

"Sexual tension is very bad for the brain," Laredo told Ranger as they met at Bloodthirsty's pen.

Ranger nodded. "I think I'll drink all day tomorrow. You should, too. That's the best way to train you for riding this beast, I do believe. Let's go get a case, and we'll both go at it. That way, when you finally do ride him, you won't remember how stupid you looked when Bloodthirsty flings you into the next county, and I won't remember the shame and embarrassment of my brother's unfortunate rendezvous with the dirt." He grimaced. "So much for Jefferson pride."

"We gotta find Tex." Laredo glanced around, frowning. "Where do you think he is? He wasn't back at Miss Delilah's."

Ranger shrugged. "Think he's across the street."

"Why do you think that?"

His brother jerked his head toward an empty stall. Suspiciously, Laredo went to peer inside.

There was a pair of pink panties lying in the straw

that said "Make My Day" in silver-studded letters. In fact, the tiny stud letters were about all that made the panties classify as a garment; there wasn't much fabric to brag about.

Laredo blinked. "They're kind of see-through."

"Yeah. You have to kick them over to read the back. It says 'And My Night Too.'" Ranger laughed. "That scalawag."

"Hmm." Laredo felt a little sad. Tex didn't have any conscience, no guilt. He knew how to eat from the Garden of Good and Evil without repercussions. Katy had been in Laredo's room, looking like sweet heaven—and all Laredo had done was stand there like a goon.

"Don't feel bad," Ranger told him. "You and Tex are total opposites. You only look alike. But inside you're so different, you'd probably be schizo if you hadn't been split into twins."

"Yes, but he's the settled one, the gardener, the grower of buds. I'm the rebel, the James Dean. But I've never had trouble with women before," Laredo said, worried. "They like me, and I like them."

"Well, Katy's got you spooked. It's because you like her for serious."

"I do not like her for serious." Laredo shook his head. "She…she's too smart for me."

"One day you'll get it together, maybe," Ranger assured him. "You'll find the moment, and you'll get it right, and when you do, I don't want to have to hear you babble about it for weeks on end. Just enjoy it, and don't screw it up."

"Screw it up?" Laredo went pale. "I don't know if I can enjoy it if I'm worried about screwing up. I think you just gave me my first case of performance anxiety, and I don't even know what I'm performing."

Ranger grinned. "For your first performance, you're going to hang on to this bull for eight seconds, or at least long enough to make yourself a winner in Katy's eyes. Then you're going to let her reward you for a job well done."

Laredo followed his brother out of the barn. "And if that's not how the performance goes?"

"Then you don't get a curtain call. You get to move onto the next Big Thing."

"That's right." Laredo told himself he felt better about that, but strangely the thought made him feel something altogether different.

Performance anxiety had just kicked up another notch.

"SEE?" HANNAH SAID. "I told you Laredo wasn't going over to the enemy." They watched as the two men got into Laredo's truck and drove away. "Don't be such a fraidy-cat."

"I'm not." But she was, Katy acknowledged to herself.

"Okay, here's the deal. When he's done riding on Saturday, you take him back down to the creek and you finish what you started before the wild boys rode in to the rescue," Hannah instructed. "After that, you can plan your future."

"Future?"

"Whether this is a spring fling for you or something serious. Whether it's Duke University, or the cowboy for you." Hannah smiled, pleased with her advice.

"I'll miss you when I go, Hannah," Katy told her. "I never had a real best friend before, and it feels good. You're so much like a sister to me."

"Hey," Hannah said, her funky-punky hair totally awry. "Don't get mushy on me. The way I see it, I'm going to lose you, either to Duke or to Malfunction Junction. It's to my benefit to do everything I can to help you and Laredo break through this barrier of reluctance you've built. Both of you. I've got to tell you," Hannah said with a sigh, "you're both so prickly around each other, it's starting to jangle my chi."

Katy followed her friend back inside. "Rest your chi. I'm going to sleep in my own bed," she said. "I have a feeling Laredo and Ranger will be gone for a long time."

WHEN KATY AWAKENED, she had the unbearable sensation of being smothered. Something was crushing her, and it was huge, and no matter which way she tried to wiggle, it had left her no room to escape.

Her mouth was open for air, so at least her trachea wasn't squished, she rationalized. It was dark in her room, too dark to see anything, but her panic subsided when she recognized Laredo's scent. Macho. But still on top of her.

"Laredo!" she whispered urgently. "Get off!"

He snored in her ear.

She tried to push him.

He didn't budge.

It wasn't all bad having the cowboy in her bed and on top of her, but this wasn't the way she'd dreamed it would happen. With a muffled grunt, she managed to pull one arm free.

"Laredo," she said, tapping on his shoulder.

Bare shoulder, she realized.

He snored again.

She moved her hand below the sheet and tapped at the bottom of his spine. "Laredo," she said more softly, not really wanting him to wake up now.

It gave her an excuse to tap just a few inches lower, just enough to tell whether—

She squeezed her eyes shut, prayed for bravery and traced a few inches lower to his buttocks.

He was buck naked. Lying on top of her.

And from the feel of frontally aligned matters, he was now fully awake.

Laredo didn't move, keeping his face buried in the pillow. Katy's tap-tapping had awakened him in every sense of the word. He knew it was Katy because no one else would be sleeping in her bed.

He just hadn't realized he'd laid himself on her when he'd crashed into bed like a falling tree. Surely he'd lain *beside* her and then rolled over on her.

His heartbeat seemed to triple. She felt so soft and small underneath him. The gentlemanly thing to do would be to get off her right now...but he had a massive erection, which he was hoping would go away any second, before she noticed.

He really did not want her to notice.

Problem was, he was pretty sure she couldn't miss it, since it was pressing against her lower region. Her female anatomy. The place where "Make My Day" underwear would be, if she were the type of girl who wore such, but she wasn't, and that was his biggest problem of all.

Her breath caught in a gasp, and he realized he was busted. She *knew*.

He was pretty certain that no matter how far Bloodthirsty threw him, his embarrassment couldn't come close to what he was now feeling.

There were two options open to a man with an obvious predicament of desire: he could apologize, get up and vacate the room—and probably the premises—for good.

Or he could act like it was nothing out of the ordinary, roll over and go back to sleep.

They didn't have to discuss it.

Suddenly he felt her hand, the one that had been tap-tap-tapping its way down his backside, make its way around his hip and underneath, between them. His surprise made him arch, and she caught him in her small, delicate hand.

"Oh, my," she said on a whisper. "I had no idea."

He hadn't, either. He was going to die if he didn't get inside her quick. There was a Lonely Hearts train running on the tracks outside—no the train was in his head, pushing all rational thought out of his mind. He couldn't bed Katy. She would regret it if he took her because he'd be her first, and he had no intention of being here past Saturday.

There wasn't a woman on earth who didn't want a man to hang around, even if she said otherwise. Especially not a virgin.

But her hand was gently squeezing, and the last of his sanity began to drain away. "Katy," he said on a groan.

"Yes?" she asked, somewhere near his ear.

It all felt too good. "Sweetheart, I want you real bad, and if you don't let go, I'm going to lose my mind."

And you're going to lose your virginity, he didn't add.

She hesitated, her hand relaxing. He tried to take a deep breath, to push back the demand his body was begging for.

"All right," she said. "I understand."

She released him, and he rolled away. She got out of the bed. Her retreat was so swift and so sudden he opened his mouth to complain.

But she was gone.

"Damn it," he said. "Damn it to hell!"

He'd only been mildly out of sorts when he'd gone to drink a few beers with Ranger, but now he was really out of sorts. And a whole keg of beer wouldn't put out the fire engulfing him. Even his mouth had dried out from erotic heat. She'd felt so good underneath him! So pliable and warm and sweet…yet once again he'd let her slip away.

And she'd sounded so disappointed it nearly killed him.

"YOU BOZO," Ranger said when he complained about it the next day. "Maybe you've forgotten what to do to a willing woman."

"That's the trouble!" Laredo glared at his brother. "She doesn't understand what she's willing to do!"

"Sounds like she does."

"I mean, she…Katy's special. She's different."

"Oh," Ranger said on an enlightened note. "She's—"

"Yes!" Laredo glared harder. "Yes, she is. And I think she should stay that way, seeing as how it's only me she's trying to give it to."

"Hmm," Ranger said thoughtfully. "That does muddy the waters a bit. I'd have to recommend that you leave that opportunity unexplored."

Laredo's heart sank as the voice of common sense jibed with his own gut reaction. "Me, too."

"After all, you have nothing to offer her."

"Nope," Laredo agreed, shaking his head.

"She could do much better, first off."

"I know," he said glumly.

"So forget about her," Ranger told him.

"I'm trying. She's just so darn cute, though."

"You know, once passion gets ahold of you, bro,

it's gonna eat a hole in you big enough to fit itself into.''

''I think I'm already there. I feel like Jerry could drive his rig through me.''

''Listen.'' Ranger clapped him on the shoulder. ''Go home. To Malfunction Junction.''

''Why?'' Laredo stared at his brother.

''You're in way over your head. You can't ride this damn bull, anyway. All they need is an eight-second guy, and that would be me. Or Tex. Not you.''

His throat dried out; his stomach clenched. ''I'm not a quitter.''

''No, but you shouldn't have said yes in the first place. Only reason you did was to show off. But you didn't know you were going to fall for Katy, and you didn't know she was, you know—'' Ranger cleared his throat delicately ''—untouched. And so, it's best if you move on. If you don't go home, at least move on, and keep looking for that Big Thing you're wanting to do. This is not it.''

Laredo closed his eyes, pressing his fingers against his eyelids. ''I think I'm falling in love.''

''I know it, you dope. Fortunately, Katy doesn't realize it. While there's still a piece of your heart that's ambivalent, get gone. Otherwise you're going to end up making love to that little gal. And you'll do something stupid after that, like get her pregnant—''

''I know how to wear a condom, thank you,'' Laredo snapped.

"Finer men than you have worn the raincoat only to find themselves at a shower nine months later. That'd be baby shower," he emphasized.

"I get it. I don't think you're right. I think I can stay here another night and ride that bull and stay away from Katy."

"And then?" Ranger asked.

"And then ride away and forget it."

"Not to doubt you, bro, but there are clues that tell me different."

"Name one," Laredo invited.

"You ran over here with your zipper unzipped, for one."

Laredo glanced down at his jeans, making a swift adjustment. "That doesn't mean a thing. It was dark on the stairwell, and I didn't want to turn on the light and wake everyone up as I passed their doors, and I was trying not to kill myself by falling down the stairs when I left."

Ranger laughed. "Whatever."

"Name another clue."

"Where did you sleep, if not in Katy's room? After the incident, I mean."

"In the upstairs den. Or TV room. Whatever you want to call it. I bunked on the sofa."

"Why'd you fall asleep on her in the first place? Just a question that leads up to clue number two."

Laredo thought about the softness under him he'd awakened to. "Guess I was tired, or I'd had too much to drink, and I got in the bed I'd been sleeping in. I didn't know she was there."

"But you ended up sleeping on top of her. Even in your subconscious, you want to be with her. Right on top of her, to be specific." Ranger grinned at him. "And anyway, all you have to do is say 'Katy,' and your nostrils flare. You look like you're going to explode any second." Ranger snickered, shaking his head. "I don't think I've ever seen anybody with the hots as bad as you've got them. You're radioactive, man."

When she'd held him in her soft, little hand, Laredo had felt positively nuclear. He rubbed his face, thinking over his choices. "I can't not ride the bull. You hellish beast," he said to Bloodthirsty.

"You're in hell, but it has nothing to do with any bull other than what you're spouting."

"I can do this. I am bigger than myself." Laredo brightened. "That's my new mission statement."

"Being bigger than yourself?" Ranger leaned against the rail. "Think of it this way. You won't be able to make love to Katy once this bull stomps your gizzards out of you, so it won't matter."

Laredo felt himself go chilly all over. "None of you became impotent from getting thrown."

Ranger laughed. "We knew how to land. You're a virgin at bull riding. She's a virgin at lovemaking. One brings you pain, and one brings you sheer joy." He shrugged. "Let me know if you want to back out. I'll make your excuses."

Laredo straightened. "A Jefferson never quits. If

I did that, then I'd be…like Maverick." He couldn't bring himself to say "Dad."

"Yeah, well." Ranger sighed. "We're all running from those demons."

Chapter Eleven

"And then?" Hannah asked with interest the next morning at the breakfast table.

"And then he disappeared like a puff of smoke, but I think even smoke hangs around longer," Katy said. "He vamoosed."

"After you massaged him." Hannah grinned like mad.

"You're not listening. I didn't really get to massage him. I tried to imagine what a Never Lonely Cut-N-Gurls might do if she were in my—"

"Bed with a hunky cowboy," Hannah said gleefully.

"I just tried to act like I knew what I was doing. Obviously, I don't." She scratched her head. "Maybe I squeezed him too tight."

Hannah wheezed and put her head down on her arms.

Katy couldn't eat. She hadn't been able to see Laredo's face when he'd hit the door, but any man who could sprint that quickly was setting a record for escape.

"I don't think you can squeeze a man too tight *there*," Hannah said. "I mean, maybe, but if he didn't say ouch, you're probably safe."

"Really?" Katy brightened.

"Oh, brother." Hannah rolled her eyes. "If I was a matchmaker, I have to admit I wouldn't try to pair the two of you up. I'd never make my commission."

"If you're trying to make me feel better, you're doing a lousy job."

"Didn't you ever have any boyfriends? Fool around at all? Back seat of someone's car? Anything?"

"I was caring for my parents. And studying. I studied a lot."

"Clearly not anatomy, Miss Brainiac." Hannah finger-combed her hair.

"What would you have done in my place?"

"Exactly what you did. Except…when he tried to move, I might not have let go."

Katy gasped. "Are you saying I should have just hung on to his…his—"

"He couldn't have left then," Hannah pointed out.

Katy was speechless. "I didn't want to hurt him. He wanted to leave. I wouldn't think it's ladylike to…try to keep him there by holding on to his— This is so confusing."

"I'm teasing. Relax." Hannah patted her hand. "There's a couple of positive clues here."

"Could you point them out? And hand me a magnifying glass?"

Hannah ignored that. "First, he had an erection."

"I heard men get those about fifty times a day. How is that special?"

Hannah shrugged. "I think that's a male-oriented myth. Their pants would look like they were keeping a jack-in-the-box inside their underwear if it were true. In Laredo's case, he has demonstrated that he clearly does not find you offensive."

"Can we get to clue number two? Because I don't think clue number one was all that decisive," Katy asked.

Hannah nodded. "Clue number two is pretty obvious, actually. He hasn't left town."

Katy stared at her.

"Well, he doesn't have to ride tomorrow, Katy. No one's paying him. He's not under a legal and binding contract. The only reason a newbie bull rider hangs around to get tossed off a bull is because there's someone he wants to impress. So I think Laredo wants to impress you." She took a bite of egg and then a drink of orange juice. "What I can't figure out," Hannah said, "is if he ever plans to make a move."

"I don't think so," Katy said dolefully. "He calls me sweetheart, though."

"Sweetheart's good," Hannah said, "but he's still gone tomorrow afternoon. Sweetheart."

Katy nodded. "He'll change, but I won't." She looked at Hannah. "He rides a bull for the first time.

But I don't do anything for the first time. And I'll never know for certain whether I'm…sexually normal.''

Frigid was not a tag she wanted to keep.

If she'd ever actually been frigid, she was pretty certain Laredo was the man to change her.

''I'd say you're toast on the lovemaking issue unless there's a miracle or a change of heart,'' Hannah agreed. ''And I'd bank on the miracle before Laredo having a change of heart where your virginity is concerned.''

She just had to talk to him, Katy decided. She would tell him how she felt about being with him. It wasn't as if she said, If you ride this bull, I'll sleep with you. What he needed to know was that…somehow she had the funny feeling that he was meant to be her first.

Of course, he wouldn't want to hear that she thought she was falling for him. That would get in the way of his plans for the big thing. He wouldn't lay a finger on her then—forget the virginity issue.

So she would tell him. No more hiding behind politeness. No more ladylike silence and waiting for him to make the first move.

It was now or a lifetime of redefining *frigid*.

But the next time Katy saw Laredo, it was Saturday.

And he was in the chute, slated to ride Bad-Ass Blue for the Never Lonely Cut-N-Gurls.

For the enemy.

Chapter Twelve

Katy couldn't believe her ears when she heard Laredo's name and Bad-Ass Blue's called together. Beside her, Hannah gasped, as did the other Lonely Hearts women. The humiliation for all of them was fairly complete. Practically everyone who knew the Jefferson brothers had turned out to watch Laredo on his virgin bull ride. Even the ten women who'd gone to set up shop in Union Junction had returned for this event. Mimi was here, too, with her new fiancé, Brian O'Flannigan. They'd even brought Mimi's father, Sheriff Cannady, along for the charitable fun.

But now Katy felt like she couldn't pull breath inside her. Laredo riding for the Never Lonely Cut-N-Gurls? How could Marvella steal their cowboy—particularly Katy's cowboy? The bigger question was *how* had she? What allure would have been enough to make Laredo susceptible?

Sitting in the stands, surrounded by now-blurred people—even more people were attending this second rodeo than the first—Katy had been so nervous. She'd gotten Laredo into this; she'd been praying that he'd be fine. What were the stats on first-time riders? Did they stay on? Get broken and stomped?

She'd hardly been able to bear the thought of it.

But when the announcer had called Laredo's name, it was Katy who got broken and stomped.

Her heart was in shocked pieces, more pieces than when Stanley had dumped her at the altar for her best friend.

ON THE BACK of Bad-Ass Blue, Tex barely heard his twin's name called as rider. There was no time to correct anyone. Beneath him, the bull was bunching and trying to kick, just itching to get out of the stall where he could run free and do his damnedest to toss the cowboy on top of him.

He tightened the rope around his gloved hand, shoved his hat down on his head one more time, put his arm up and nodded.

LAREDO HEARD HIS NAME called for the wrong bull, but he was dealing with a bigger problem. Bloodthirsty Black had definitely gotten up on the wrong side of the pen this morning, and though his brother Crockett had come early to paint the bull's hooves, the bull had decided he wasn't going to put up with that nonsense, either.

This bull had gotten more ornery with each passing hour. They'd had a helluva time getting the hooves decorated for the contest. This was especially important to Laredo, because he was desperately afraid he wasn't going to win the bull riding contest, and he wanted to bring home a win of some kind. He and Crockett had argued over creative design—Crockett was on a nudes-only kick—but Laredo felt that was inappropriate considering the salon for which he was riding as knight in shining armor. Besides, he'd told Crockett, the type of detail with which Crockett liked to paint his nudes would probably lose some artistic power once translated onto a bull's hooves.

So in the process of arguing over the matter of nudes versus the roses that Laredo thought would be a blue ribbon winner, Bloodthirsty Black took a horn to the paint cans and Crockett's rump, neatly lifting him a foot into the air and scooping him out of the pen onto the concrete floor.

It was Bull-1, Cowboys-0, Laredo thought grimly, but no bull was going to get the best of him.

The bull was not appeased and sensed he was in the company of a greenhorn. After that, every time Laredo came near the bull, Bloodthirsty Black let out a bellow, which might have been a victory yell, and it might have been a warning. Either way, it was making Laredo more nervous than he'd previously been.

The beer he'd drunk the night before as part of Ranger's suggested training was no longer sitting comfortably in his body. Knight in shining armor, he reminded himself, staring at the painted bull. Unfortunately, his armor felt dastardly dull today.

Crockett did a swift, impressive press-on design of vivid bluebonnets, which was his artistic compromise to Laredo's suggestion of roses. "They remind me of nudes," Crockett told Laredo, "they're pear-shaped and lush and beautiful."

"What-freaking-ever," Laredo said, his mood totally sour. The bluebonnet renderings looked really cool on Bloodthirsty's midnight hooves, and Laredo had to take his hat off to Crockett's swift application of paint on waxed paper which he pressed onto each hoof the second Bloodthirsty decided to glare at Laredo. But they in no way looked like nudes to Laredo, and right now, he'd have given anything to be in a place with nudes and no bulls. "Miss Delilah should be real pleased with your work, Crockett."

Crockett beamed at the praise. "His hooves are going to flash as they fly through the air in the ring."

Laredo glared at Crockett as he shrugged into the shirt Miss Delilah had given him to wear. "Why did you drag everybody from Union Junction to the rodeo? I just wanted your artistry, not a convention."

"We wouldn't have missed your first ride, Laredo, even if we think you're brainless for doing it."

"Yeah, well. You must have looked like a convoy tearing over here with everybody. And what's up with Mason? He looks like some unattractive bug species just flew into his mouth." Laredo peered into the arena where he could see the Union Junction crowd taking up a full grandstand.

"Mimi's fiancé tagged along. It's not that we

don't like Brian, it's just that he seems to have a rude effect on Mason.''

"How so?'' Laredo tightened his belt.

"Mason sees Brian, Mason gets ruder. Or annoyingly silent. We can't decide which is worse.''

Laredo looked up. "It's not like Mason was winning any prizes for personality to start with.''

"It's getting worse, bro. In the past couple days, Mason seemed to have come to grips with Mimi's engagement, but then we got the wedding invitation, and—''

Laredo held up a hand. "Don't tell me any more. I don't want my brother to be the last thing on my mind before I get squished. I'm going to the chute. How do I look?''

"Like you're about to die,'' Crockett said cheerfully. "And not too happy about it, either. Hey, you really like that little girl, don't you?''

"What little girl?'' Laredo glowered at his brother, arranging his steely game face for the upcoming showdown. If the game face worked on Crockett, maybe it would impress Bloodthirsty.

But Crockett laughed. "You're just like Mason,'' he said. "They say actions speak louder than words, but I never knew that the one who was acting could be totally deaf to themselves.''

"Huh?'' Laredo glowered harder. "Paint fumes get to you?''

"Yep, just like Mason,'' Crockett said on a sigh. "Showing your emotions through physical engagement.''

"Whereas you paint your emotions, and since nudes are your favorite artistic topic, can I assume you're hornier than a mallard in May?"

The smile slipped off Crockett's face. "And that's just what Mason would have said. You're turning into him."

"No, I'm not." Laredo turned to walk away. "That's precisely why I left the Malfunction Junction."

"Good luck," Crockett said to Laredo's retreating back. "And not necessarily with you," he told Bloodthirsty. "Whew! Talk about deprivation. If anybody's got it bad, it's him. If you break something on him, I'm painting mating mallards all over his cast!"

WHY TEX HAD DECIDED to ride for the Never Lonely Cut-N-Gurls, Laredo wasn't certain. Nor did he have time to find out anything more than his twin's score of an eighty-nine.

Not bad, but not unbeatable, either. Of course, Tex had a lot of experience, and Laredo had none.

Bloodthirsty was brought into the chute, and he was helped onto the trapped bull.

Oh, hellfire. What was he doing here? Pull rope tight around glove, mash down hat for good measure, be grateful to the four cowboys trying to keep this bull from breaking his legs against the chute walls, hope Katy's watching, hope he stayed on this stupid bull, he *was* going to stay on this stupid bull—

He heard his name called as rider—mix-up on the names, Jerry the truck driver explained as he played announcer—but a Jefferson was a Jefferson and how lucky was Lonely Hearts Station to have a pair of strapping twins from Union Junction here to help them out in their charitable endeavors.

None of that mattered to Laredo at the moment. The "Make My Day" panties had probably had a lot to do with his twin riding for the opposing salon. He wouldn't take offense to that, but if he lost to Tex, he'd probably have to thrash him later for the sake of his ego.

"He pulls to the left," Cissy's voice reminded him. "And then, just when you lean, he jerks to the right with a mean midair kick. Every time."

Tex had said he didn't think the bull pulled to the left. Laredo took a deep breath and leaned to anticipate the jerk to the right.

Why hadn't the damn gate opened? Laredo nodded, remembering at the last second that he was supposed to do so. The chute door swung open, and he was dimly aware of a rodeo clown clinging to the side of the arena before Bloodthirsty burst out, wringing hellfire from Hades and flashing bluebonnet-painted hooves.

KATY'S HEART LEAPED inside her as Bloodthirsty Black flung himself from the chute. He was an immense bull—and the rider on his back appeared to be Laredo. She clasped her hands together, praying harder than she'd ever prayed. Eight seconds—that was all the Lonely Hearts Salon needed. Eight seconds—please don't let Laredo get hurt.

Two seconds later Laredo went flying off Bloodthirsty Black, landing gracefully for a man who was thrown boots-over-head. But the bull wasn't through with him, and having a taste for Jefferson brother butt after horning Crockett, elected to do the same to Laredo. Laredo went flying into a post, the bull was shooed away by the clown, and Katy was already running down the steps before the Jefferson brothers vaulted en masse from the grandstand.

"WELL," MARVELLA SAID with a satisfied grin, as the Never Lonely Hearts cowboy went flying. She was watching from the stands across the arena from her sister. "Who would have imagined twins? You stole the wrong cowboy, Cissy."

"I thought it was Laredo," Cissy said hotly, wondering why Tex hadn't mentioned in the entire night that they'd spent together that he wasn't Laredo. But now that she thought about it, their time together had been very silent, very passionate and very, very satisfying. She got shivers all over thinking about it. In her newly formed opinion, Tex was all man and no bull, and if she ever got the chance to make love with the wrong cowboy again, he wouldn't have to ask twice.

Of course, he wouldn't ask again. Men like that went for sweet girls, delicate untouched girls like Katy Goodnight. They liked their fun and adventure, but in the end they married a Madonna. The real kind. And she was no Madonna.

It didn't matter that she'd wanted a different life. It didn't matter that she wished she'd known about Delilah and her girls before she signed on with Marvella. She'd been desperate, and she'd reached out to take the hand that had saved her when she was drowning, and there was no turning back. She had secrets—eight of them—and she could never forget that.

She stared at Katy Goodnight rushing to Laredo's side, and the pit of Cissy's stomach turned with empathy. Inside, all she could think of was how glad and relieved she was that she hadn't stolen Katy's cowboy. No matter how wonderful the lovemaking had been, there had been a tinge of regret for what she was doing.

"It doesn't matter," Marvella said with delight. "Even if you didn't humiliate them by stealing their rider, you appear to have lured the only cowboy who *could* ride. And believe me, that's a job well done, my dear."

No, it's not, Cissy thought, watching as a doctor aided Laredo to his feet. Something was wrong with him. And it was all her fault. She had given him bad advice at first—though later she'd corrected it. But the nagging voice of conscience wouldn't go away.

THE GATE MONEY was considerable this time, almost double the first rodeo, money that Lonely Hearts

Station desperately needed for the city coffers. Street repair and some renovations to the cafeteria were tops on the list the city fathers—and Mother Delilah—had in mind.

The prize money and the buckle went to the Never Lonely Cut-N-Gurls, again. But that wasn't the part that had Katy in tears. She'd gotten Laredo on the back of that bull—and now he had a concussion.

A slight one, the doctor at the hospital said. What could be termed level one, and thankfully the CT scan was normal. But he still had enough of a concussion that he needed rest.

He'd sure been talking stupid there for a while, something that had straightened the hair on Katy's arms. Something about his dad. Where was his dad? Where was his dad? Over and over again, until Mason had finally barked at him to relax. But then Laredo had started babbling about the winning nudes. Did the nudes win? The blue nudes? Did the nudes win?

Tex finally told Laredo that a blue nude would win anytime, and would he please rest his mouth?

Katy had felt terrible for Laredo. It was all her fault. She'd wanted a win for Delilah so badly, wanted to be a help and thank her for all Delilah'd done for her that she'd risked this cowboy's life.

Fortunately, his head had cleared an hour later, and he never mentioned blue nudes again. Now they were all standing outside the hospital, deciding how to organize the going-home exodus. During the wait for Laredo to be examined, some of the Jefferson brothers had sneaked out to Laredo's truck and unearthed the beer out of the now-iceless cooler. Mimi and her fiancé had long since gone home. She said she needed to check on her father, who had left early.

"Laredo can ride back with me to Union Junction," Mason said.

It was probably for the best, though Katy's heart sank a little.

Laredo glanced at her, shaking his head and then wincing. "I'm staying here," Laredo said, "if Miss Delilah will have me."

"Of course!" Delilah replied instantly. "We should nurse you back to health!"

But it was Katy he was looking at while he waited for an answer. "I can find someplace other than your room," he said. "The upstairs den sofa is fine."

"Absolutely not. Hannah and I can bunk together for a few more days, until you're feeling better."

"I'm not the champion you were hoping for, Katy."

She looked into his eyes and saw the disappointment he was suffering. "Come on," she said. "Tex brought your truck. He can ride back with one of your brothers."

"Tex, give Katy my keys," Laredo instructed. "She's going to drive me ho—um, she's going to drive me back to Miss Delilah's."

"Are you sure you don't want to come back with us?" Tex asked, handing the keys over, anyway.

"I've only started on the first leg of my journey to doing a Big Thing. So the leg has a small joint in it I wasn't expecting. It's not enough to make me put my tail between my legs and head home."

"You *should* head home," Mason interjected. "Helga can take care of you. Katy needs to be working, I'm sure, not playing nurse to a cowboy who shouldn't have tried to ride what he didn't know anything about."

Laredo scowled. "I'm fine, Mason. And let me be the first to inform you, since Frisco Joe didn't seem to enlighten you, I'd rather be nursed by Hitler than Helga. We all would."

Frisco Joe put his arm around Annabelle, who was holding baby Emmie. "Helga *is* Hitler, in woman's attire. Did you know he had a thing for cross-dressing? And that it's rumored he's not really dead? Look closely at Helga's face, and you'll see a striking—"

"Enough!" Mason cut in, his tone allowing no further argument. "Your manners are showing, both of you. Helga took very good care of you when you were dumb enough to bust your leg."

All the Jefferson boys rolled their eyes, knowing full well it was Helga's ministrations that sent Frisco Joe running to Lonely Hearts Station to seek shelter with Annabelle Turnberry, now Jefferson.

"Thanks all the same, Mason. I'm staying here," Laredo stated. "It's safer, believe me."

Katy's eyes were locked on Laredo. "If you're sure about this, let me get you back to the salon.

The doctor says it's very important that you don't scramble your brains again for three months, and that you rest completely for forty-eight hours.''

''I need it,'' he said. ''Because I'm asking for a rematch in a week's time.''

Chapter Thirteen

"You can't be serious," Katy told Laredo once she was behind the wheel of his truck. "The doctor told you not to hit your head again for at least three months. You'll end up with Troy Aikman syndrome."

It didn't matter, Laredo knew. Conquering Big Things had to do with bravery. Commitment. Grit. And not running out when things got rough.

"And our salon did win the Best Painted Hooves contest," Katy continued. "We blew them clean out of the water on that one."

Of course the prize money for that was smaller, but Crockett's rendition had brought him a lot of attention, which he totally deserved since his own brothers were the first to rag him on his artistic endeavors.

No matter how much they really were developing an artist's appreciation and a voyeur's eye for his nudes.

"But that was Crockett," Laredo said. "It didn't have anything to do with me."

"You asked him to paint for us. That's something."

Katy stopped at a single-light intersection, and Laredo put his hand over hers on the wheel. "Katy, you don't understand. I know I can stay on next time. And I aim to prove it."

"Well, any notoriety you bring to Miss Delilah helps the price of her bull," Katy said slowly. "Goodness knows the gate take was up, and we even had some regional photographers doing some articles, so our tourism will probably improve—"

"Katy, it's the least I can do."

"Why, Laredo?" She stared at him. "Why do you want to help us so much?"

"Because it's the right thing to do. Helping to save a small town in a struggling economy is worthwhile as far as I'm concerned. As soon as I get the chance, I'm going to tell Tex he's a rat for riding against me."

"He said that the Cut-N-Gurls didn't have a rider. Which makes sense, if you think about it, Laredo. All these people had bought tickets. They would have been disappointed if we hadn't had the rodeo with the headline event." Besides the marquee re-match, several lesser bulls had been ridden. There'd been a calf catch, as well as a table of cowboys playing chicken to see who would be last to vacate their seat before a bull charged them. It had been a huge success. "Maybe the Cut-N-Gurls weren't even being sneaky this time," Katy said.

"I may have seen evidence to the contrary. Hot pink with silver lettering, but never mind that right now. I just want to get in bed."

She felt her face pinken as she parked the truck in back of the salon. "Here we are."

They went upstairs, Katy leading the way. "Can I get you something to drink?"

"You can get me something," Laredo said, drawing her into his arms, "but a drink isn't what I had in mind."

"I don't think you should kiss me while your head isn't totally clear."

His arms locked around her. "I'm not suffering from temporary amnesia. I know full well that your name is Penny Calfcatcher."

She rolled her eyes at him. "Very funny, cowboy."

"I let you down."

"Not by half." Lifting her foot, she nudged the bedroom door closed behind them, and began to pull off the Lonely Hearts shirt Laredo was wearing. "Let's get you ready for bed."

"You're being very Helga-ish. I'm going to insist upon a winner's kiss, even though I didn't win."

She looked up at him. "Laredo, I can't. I'm too nervous. Too uncertain. When I thought you were riding for the Cut-N-Gurls, I nearly died a thousand deaths. I thought last month had repeated itself, with them stealing our cowboy. Only this time, you'd been stolen from me, just like my—'' she drooped her head ''—my ex-fiancé.''

''Katy—''

He tried to tip her chin up but she shrugged his finger away. ''You're braver than me, Laredo. Already you're itching to get back on and try again with Bloodthirsty. But I'm not a get-back-in-the-saddle girl, I guess. I want to keep both my feet firmly planted on the ground.''

He stared at her, and she had to glance away from his deep, probing gaze. His expression was puzzled and disappointed and wistful. It made her heart turn over hard in her chest. ''I'm sorry,'' she whispered. ''I really am.''

''No way would I have ever done that, Katy,'' he said softly. ''I would never have ridden for the opposing team.''

''I know. I knew that then, but seeing was believing, Laredo, if only for eight horrible seconds.'' She shook her head. ''I had no reason to imagine that the announcer was wrong, or that your twin had gone over to the other side.''

''It's not my fault,'' he told her, stroking her face. ''Katy, you're going to have to learn to trust again one day. I propose that I'm the man you should trust.''

''Why?'' she asked. ''You were supposed to leave today. Right after the rodeo. Nothing's stopping you but a concussion.''

''I could leave now. But I haven't.''

She turned her face slightly away. ''Laredo,

please don't press me. I have a thousand thoughts racing through my head, and I just don't want to…make another mistake. My heart can't take it." She took a deep breath. "Remember the fight-or-flight theory? Well, I want to stay on my flight plan. I'm finishing up my summer here, and then I'm going on to Duke where I belong. I'm going to teach science, be the best prof I can be and bury myself in academic pursuits. If I hadn't strayed from my plan in the beginning, I wouldn't have ended up a jilted woman. I'm not straying again," she said, her voice resolute as she turned back to look into his eyes.

"You really thought I would do that to you?"

"I didn't know." She couldn't look at the pain in his eyes. "I just really didn't know. The Cut-N-Gurls can be so tricky."

"Your confidence is down," he said comfortingly. "And I understand that. But, Katy, sometimes a man can't be taken in by a woman. They have to want to be. And I don't want to be taken in by those ladies. I like you."

The shell around her heart crackled a little, allowing hope to stream in. "I know you find Cissy attractive."

"Sure. Even Cissy finds Cissy attractive. But that doesn't mean I'd go there. And don't say anything about the Jefferson reputation. Tex may be my twin, but we couldn't be more different." He rubbed his chin, wondering about his brother's sudden penchant for the beauty queen temptress. "Actually, to be honest, I'm a little surprised by my brother. Tex isn't the type to fall for a girl like...well, never mind.''

"See?" she said softly. "If you're surprised about Tex, why is it so unlikely that I would have misjudged you? The Cut-N-Gurls have a focal goal, they go for it, and rarely do they not achieve it.''

"They didn't this time.''

"Maybe they seduced Tex, thinking it was you.''

"Jeez, do not even mention that around my twin. He would have a fit. His ego couldn't take it.'' Laredo laughed softly. "Even if they did, that should just confirm to you that I'm unseduceable.''

"Completely?''

"Care to find out?'' He nuzzled her nose.

"You have a concussion. Why don't you crawl into bed before you short-circuit something?''

"Maybe I will.'' He sighed suddenly, sounding tired, and sat on the edge of her bed. "Hey, Rose. What's going on in the mouse house?'' Something on the nightstand caught his eye, and slowly he picked it up. "'Lars Van Hooven, photographer, *Playboy Magazine.*''' He turned his gaze to her. "Why do you have this business card?''

She snatched it from his fingers. "No special reason. And just because you're bunking in here does not give you permission to snoop.''

He stared at her for a long moment. "You're not thinking of posing, are you?''

Starting to say no, Katy stopped herself. "I might.

They're looking for sweet, unsophisticated, country girls—''

He sat up stiff and straight. ''I don't think so.''

She automatically bristled. Okay, so she'd gone into more description than was necessary just to jerk his chain, but his attitude made her want to call Lars Van Hooven on the spot. ''Wait a minute, there, cowboy—''

''No, Katy.''

A gasp escaped her. ''Laredo, you can't tell me what to do.''

''I'm not,'' Laredo insisted. ''I'm expressing my opinion.''

''You don't get one!''

''I do, too. I'm voting no. You won't be able to do it, Katy, and anyway, if you think you want to pose nude, you can pose for me.'' He leaned back against the headboard and crossed his arms. ''In fact, you can start now.''

''What?''

''Take off your clothes and pose for me. I want to see your smiles, both horizontal and vertical.''

She frowned at him. ''I'm not undressing in front of you. And may I add that I don't like your tone? It smacks of…possessiveness or something.''

He raised a brow at her, which made her nervous.

''And besides, you're missing the point I'm trying to make.''

''Which would be what, Miss July?''

She gave him a gimlet eye. ''You rematch on that damn bull, and I pose.''

"It's a matter of pride, Katy. I know I can do it. I'd just never felt a bull beneath me before, and I didn't know what to expect. Now I do. Experience counts."

"You're wearing your experience in the shape of a dented skull. Laredo, I got you into this, and I have to be the one to say it's not worth getting yourself brained over."

"Well, you can't just say you don't like my decision for a rematch—which, I might add, the Lonely Hearts Station city fathers and mother agreed to with great interest—you're only going to pose for *Playboy* because you don't want a rematch."

"I'm going to do something daring," Katy stated. "Not daring by some girls' standards, maybe, but certainly by mine. It's my Big Thing, Laredo."

His mouth thinned into a straight, compressed line. "You're going to make me say it, aren't you?"

"Say what?" She was curious, staring at the cowboy on her bed. Golly, but he was handsome. And yet so stubborn! Now that she thought about it, Stanley was not so handsome, and rather spineless. Just the opposite of Laredo. But she hadn't known who she was looking for before, just the what, which was a belated spring fling, which then turned into a marriage proposal.

But Stanley hadn't turned out to be a spring fling. She had the experience now to know better.

However, as she stared pugilistically at Laredo, she recognized that he was even less of a spring fling than Stanley. All that claptrap Stanley had given her about staying a virgin until after they were married had come down to him desiring not her but her family connections.

"You want me to say that I won't do the rematch. But I've already said I would, and I can't back out now, because that would be reneging on the Jefferson name."

"That's what you had to say? That load of turkey trimmings?" Why had she hoped he would say something romantic, like *I'm only doing it to impress you?*

"Katy!" Laredo swung his feet over the side of the bed and stalked toward her. "You're making this very tough on me."

"I actually don't see why you should care, Laredo." Katy was only being honest. "It's my body. My life. My chance to be…uninhibited."

It appeared that he ground his teeth together. She could hear what sounded like crunching sandpaper in his mouth before he put his hands on her shoulders. "Katy Goodnight," he said, "you're far more ornery than any marquee bull. So…I'm going to go spend the night somewhere else."

SHE'D LEFT HIM with no choice, Laredo told himself as he stalked outside. For the first time, he began to feel a real headache coming on. Originally, he'd had a tender, bruised area on his head, but this went below the surface.

No one had ever infuriated him like Katy Goodnight.

For such a sweet-faced girl, she made him want to toss her down on the bed and kiss her until she said she'd do whatever he wanted her to. Mainly, not pose in a girlie mag! She was so innocent she didn't realize what men bought those magazines for. And if she thought he was going to allow her to let men see her and fulfill their sexual needs while staring at her—

"Whatcha doing?" Tex demanded from his truck bed.

"What the hell are you doing?" Laredo demanded, although it was obvious. Tex and Ranger were enjoying the brilliant starlit night, both of them sitting on top of barrels they'd retrieved from heaven knew where and drinking beer out of the still-packed cooler.

"Trying to decide if we should come in there and drag you out and take you home," Ranger said. "We're debating the points in your IQ for saying you wanted a rematch. I've got you at about seventy, but Tex says you're closer to a hundred."

Which marked him from somewhat mentally challenged to pretty much mentally challenged, depending on whose scale he cared to use. "Is that beer still warm?"

"Nah. We got some ice out of Miss Delilah's freezer and restocked the cooler. Nice chilly brewskis now," Tex said with satisfaction. "How's your head?"

"Hurting, but not necessarily from Bloodthirsty's tricks." He climbed up into the truck bed, sat on the edge of the truck and took the beer Ranger offered him. "What made you ride for the Cut-N-Gurls, Tex?"

"Sex," Ranger said, though Tex shook his head.

"Not sex. Just wanted to do a little riding again, I guess. It was for a good cause, too, and that made up my mind. However, I had no idea you'd get thrown so easily."

"Don't go easy on my pride or anything." He took a swig of beer.

"I'm not," Tex said. "What I meant was that I figured it was all good clean fun. I figured you'd stay on come hell or high water to impress Katy, and I figured without a Cut-N-Gurl rider, you wouldn't get the chance to show off."

"So you did it for me?" Laredo asked.

"Not necessarily. I really wanted to ride again. I liked being a hero." He sighed deeply. "I'd rather have been a hero for this salon. I had to take my apologies to Miss Delilah, and I sure did feel like a rat."

"You are a rat," Ranger said with a grin, "but you meant well."

"Do you like Cissy?" Laredo asked.

Tex stared at both his brothers. "She's a nice girl."

"That's it?" Laredo probed.

"Well, how do you feel about Katy?" Tex asked defensively.

"Most of the time, confused. I want her naked, I

want her pure, I want to spank her, I want to...I don't know. Marry her, maybe."

"What?" both his brothers yelped.

"Man, you hit your head harder than we thought," Tex said. "Marriage isn't a Big Thing."

"It is," Laredo said defensively. "It is if you intend for it to be forever."

Ranger put his hands behind his head. "Do we know anyone who's been married forever? Without any fooling around or trial separations? Just unending bliss?"

Tex shoved his hat back on his head. "I don't think we personally know of a documented case, but maybe they're out there. And Union Junction is so small that it's not really a representative sampling of the population."

Laredo rubbed his brow tiredly, just above where his head was throbbing. "We do know someone who's happily married. Think about it."

"Well, there's the Jenkins," Ranger offered.

"Only because the missus doesn't let the mister talk. Heaven knows what he would say if he could get a word in edgewise."

"Probably, 'Help! Help!'" Tex said. "What about the Smyths?"

"You can't count them," Ranger stated. "Mrs. Smyth was married to two men at the same time."

"She didn't know it," Laredo pointed out. "She thought one husband was dead in the war, and she remarried. But then she got divorced and married her first husband when he returned ten years later."

"Which was weird enough," Tex said with a grin, "except that then both the men remained in the house with her."

"They're wounded war vets," Laredo reminded him. "They both needed some assistance. It was a suitable arrangement all around." If a bit scandalous, he forbore to mention.

"I'll say," Tex agreed. "Maybe I'll find a wife who'll agree to let me have a second wife in the same house with us. I could dig being tended by two women."

"You'll be the walking wounded then," Ranger told him. "Plus the expense would be far worse than having two Thoroughbred racehorses, and there'd no doubt be hellacious bitching going on. Just concentrate on fertilizing your roses, Tex."

"So what about you and Hannah?" Laredo asked his brother.

"What about us?" Ranger's tone was unyielding.

"I thought maybe you liked her. Although you did go off with Cissy for a while."

Ranger shrugged. "I'm not going to like anyone. My life is fine the way it is. And I still say you should let your brains unscramble before you find yourself doing something stupid like getting married."

That's what it was, Laredo realized. He'd hit his head, and then Katy had mentioned posing nude, and he'd been attacked by paralyzing pain in his brain, and the word *marriage* had appeared as if Vanna White had turned the letters for him. The thing was, he wasn't the jealous type. Never had been. Nor had he been the possessive type. So, clearly, he *had* knocked something loose. "I think I'll turn in," he said suddenly. "The doctor said I needed forty-eight hours of good rest. And I believe her."

Ranger laughed. "We've been meaning to ask you about that doctor, by the way. She had nice long legs and some other things. Did you suffer any amnesia? Because we want to know what kind of perfume she was wearing."

Laredo grunted. The doctor in question had been a Whitney Houston look-alike, a major babe in every way. He'd never have enough amnesia to keep him from noticing a woman like her. Plus her hands had been soft and cool when she touched his head.

What he really needed a prescription for was how, despite the doctor's beauty and soft touch, he'd kept thinking about Katy's worried face peering at him as he'd lain on the arena floor.

He didn't have amnesia. He had obsession, and best he could recall, there was no cure for that.

He jumped down from the truck bed and crawled inside the cab. Then he lay down, telling himself he'd be himself after a good night's rest.

"Nighty-night," he heard Ranger call, his voice all but grinning, if voices could. "Sweet dreams."

"Shut up," Laredo muttered to himself. If he was lucky, he wouldn't dream about Katy in front of a photographer's lens, showing her charms to the whole world. She was just bossy enough to do it.

"If you rematch, I pose," she'd said.

The thought made him groan.

Sweet 'n' sour Miss Katy Goodnight had two things she was about to learn: one, he never backed down from a challenge.

He *was* going to rematch.

Second, he never backed down from a challenge.

She had to be protected from herself. And he was just the bad-ass-in-the-flesh cowboy to do it.

TEX WATCHED through the back truck window as Laredo settled down in the cab. "Do we hang around for the final showdown or do we bail?"

Ranger shrugged and swigged some beer. "You're in it up to your hips, I'd say. Mason says he can give us a few more days off, especially if we come home in the middle of the week to lend a hand. Besides, you've got to ride again."

"Uh-uh. Not me. I only ride against my brother once."

Ranger stared at him. "You didn't ride against Laredo. He rode against himself. You were just a practice partner."

"Are you suggesting I should ride again?"

"Did Laredo ask you not to?"

"No." Tex rolled his shoulders and neck uneasily. "But I should think it would be obvious that family sticks together. And we're all behind the Lonely Hearts ladies." He shook his head. "I didn't mind subbing when the rodeo was too close to be called off. But they've got time to find another cow-boy now.''

"Thing is, Laredo needs to beat you just as much as he needs to beat that bull," Ranger whispered. "Otherwise, he'll never know."

"Never know what?" Tex whispered back.

Ranger sighed. "Well, think it through. You heard all that bull Laredo gave Katy about Mason not letting him ride rodeo, didn't you?"

"Yeah." Tex scratched his forehead.

"Well, think about why he didn't just tell her the truth."

"That Mason was less keen on Laredo riding than any of us, simply because he knew he'd never come home?"

"That's just it," Ranger said. "He didn't tell Katy that. And he didn't tell her that he loved play-ing soccer. He didn't tell her that while the rest of us were getting our heads cracked open, Mason was running him from field to field. He didn't tell her that he'd actually won a scholarship and gone to college full-ride. And he sure as hell didn't tell her the real truth: that he hated rodeo with a passion, and that bulls and broncs held no appeal for him whatsoever."

"Truth be known, he was always a little bit aston-ished by our interest," Tex agreed. "Couldn't un-derstand why we enjoyed getting thrown off. And we couldn't understand why he enjoyed hanging about with a bunch of sweaty lads pouring Gatorade over each other and eating oranges."

"There you have it," Ranger said. "You see what I'm trying to tell you."

"Not really."

"He did the one thing he really had no interest in, and was even maybe a little scared of. It's his Big Thing. But he did it for Katy."

"Ohh," Tex said.

"So you have to ride. You're just about the best of the best, and if he can beat you this time—and his fear—then he's set himself up as a worthy knight for Katy."

Tex squinted at him. "How many beers have you drunk?"

"I don't know. Why?"

"Because you sound like you've drunk a case, yet somehow I'm hearing your reasoning clearly. Maybe *I've* drunk the case."

Ranger grinned at him. "Faint heart never won fair lady. Didn't you ever hear that?"

"I don't think so…. I've heard that you can't make a silk purse out of a sow's ear."

Ranger raised his brows at him. "Are you saying Laredo can't do it?"

Tex sighed. "I've got a lot of experience, Ranger. We can't hang around here forever riding a bull once a week so that Laredo can finally catch up and beat me to impress Katy."

"I know that. I don't think it'll take another week."

"And it's a really stupid, caveman, macho-guy way to woo a woman, anyway. That bodacious doc said Laredo wasn't to risk another head injury or he could really do damage. And then he'll end up at home with Helga, and then we'll have to keep him doped on smuggled prescriptions.''

''He's not wooing the woman by riding the bull. He's wooing himself. He's got to do a Big Thing.''

''You said he was doing it for Katy.''

''I said he was doing what he didn't want to do for her. The choice of weapon is for her but the battle itself, that's all his.''

Tex sighed. ''For crying out loud. And say he wins. Then what?''

Ranger got off the barrel and lay down with his head against the side. Crossing his boots, he pulled his hat down low. ''I only do analysis. To predict the future would make me a mind reader, and I'd have to be able to factor in Katy's mind set.''

''No one can predict what a woman will do,'' Tex pointed out.

''I agree. Get some sleep. We're going to be very busy tomorrow.''

''I'd rather sleep in a bed.''

Ranger sighed. ''Me, too. But Laredo's not sleeping inside, and that tells me something's not going all that well in the land of romance. So we gotta sleep out here and keep an eye on him.''

''He won't sleepwalk.''

''No, but someone might walk on him in his sleep.''

Tex straightened. ''Hey, the Cut-N-Gurls won't

shanghai him. They're not that way. I think everybody's got them all wrong.''

''Do you like Cissy Kisserton?''

''No,'' he denied. ''Do you?''

''If I did, you'd never have had a shot at her. By the way, I was pretty impressed that you pulled an 89 after being up all night.''

Tex stared at his brother's lowered hat suspiciously. ''Who said I was up all night?''

''Just a hunch.''

''Keep your hunches to yourself. I'm not interested. And,'' Tex said, hunkering down next to his brother, ''don't even get started, because if I ever do have a grand romance, you're going to be the last to know about it!''

''I hope so,'' Ranger said mildly.

''So do I.'' Tex studied the stars for a moment. ''Want to know a secret?''

''Not really.''

''Marvella's bull isn't as mean as Bloodthirsty. In fact, he was a downright creampuff.''

Ranger's hat moved back as he pushed it so that he could stare at Tex. ''What are you saying?''

''I'm saying that there are bulls born to make a rider look good, and there are bulls born to make a rider look bad. Bad-Ass Blue made me look good. I really didn't have to do anything except hold on for eight. No trick shots, no low punches.''

''Not a marquee bull?''

Tex shrugged. ''Maybe Blue was having an off day. That bull's supposed to be meaner than mean.''

"Says who?"

"Says everyone. Besides, the judges can tell when you're getting a good ride. He looks good. He looks mean. And he sure can run and kick with the best of them. But he doesn't have the lust for kill that Bloodthirsty has. Sure, he's mad and all. But he's lacking the fundamental tricks to be a nasty ride. Bloodthirsty's not a ride at all. He's a one-way suicide ticket."

"We could switch you," Ranger said quickly. "No one was the wiser when they announced the wrong riders this time. No one would notice next time."

"Nope. No way. Laredo would never allow it. You said it yourself, this is his Big Thing. Fact is, this is a holy war between Laredo and the same thing we're all grappling with."

Silence met that comment as they thought about growing up without parents most of the time. For some of the brothers it had been just about all of the time. It hadn't been terrible, but Mason was outnumbered and outmanned. He deserved a Purple Heart. Laredo had been the go-to guy when Mason had been funky.

Of course, the downside of this was that if Laredo was blowing a fuse now, then Mason was way overdue.

Tex sighed. "Nope, my twin's got himself set square on the horns of his own dilemma, and there are only two things I can see happening here. One, he wins. Two, he loses. Both are out of our control."

But with a trick bull and a woman who'd sent him to his truck for the night, it seemed Laredo was in it up to his ears.

Tex was relieved he wasn't in his twin's boots.

But we'd appreciate it if you wouldn't—which

truthfully stuck in her craw—that if that's what

it meant to the town—

You all go right ahead now, little lady, we know.

Chapter Fourteen

Delilah was more worried about the rematch than she let on. The calls from surrounding city papers had been gratifying. They'd even had a few offers of corporate sponsorship from some big-city restaurants. Bloodthirsty, it seemed, was garnering quite the reputation. For that matter, bookings for haircuts in her salon were up by twenty percent, and all from city folk interested in having their hair done by one of Lonely Hearts Station's infamous salons.

There was only one way to beat Marvella at her own game, and that was all that was on Delilah's mind today. It was past time she and her sister had a little chat. She could send someone in her place; Delilah being a town councilwoman, and it being town business, someone else on the council *could* talk to Marvella.

But this had become personal, now that Laredo had gotten hurt, and as far as she was concerned, the buck stopped with her. "I'm going to see Marvella,'' she told Jerry, who was sitting in the kitchen icing some cookies for her.

He never paused in what he was doing. ''I'll send out the rescue squad if you're not back in an hour, but there's two things you should know.''

''What?'' She turned to him with a waiting expression on her face.

''One, it's a volunteer rescue squad. We don't pay folks around here like the big city pays its emergency workers.''

''Fair enough. Second?''

''Being that it's volunteer, the squad will most likely consist of me and those Jefferson boys asleep in Laredo's truck out there. I'm fixing to run them out some of these cookies.''

''For breakfast?''

''They're just like doughnuts in my opinion,'' Jerry said cheerfully, ''and they'll sit right fine on guts full of beer.''

Delilah shuddered. ''If you change your mind and decide to make breakfast for our champions, there are eggs and biscuits in the fridge.''

''Delilah?''

''Yes?''

''How did you feel about Tex riding for the opposing team?''

''I felt rotten about it when I thought Laredo was on their bull, for Katy's sake. When I realized it was Tex, I felt fine. The Jefferson brothers are bringing business to my salon, Jerry, and to this town that I love. I can't complain about that.''

Jerry grinned. "They sure are bringing in the women from far and away. Most of the reservations we took today were from women new to town, and all wanting to look beautiful for the rodeo. And all wanting to know who was riding this weekend."

"Ah." Delilah smiled and closed the door. She was a smart businesswoman. There was opportunity in a situation that had been out of her hands for too long.

It was time to start taking it back.

"Marvella," she called, throwing open the Never Lonely Cut-N-Gurls Salon door. About twenty employees and that many customers stopped everything they were doing, which, as far as she could see, was mainly inhabit a Jacuzzi and enjoy some masseuse attention. She was pretty certain all she had to do was send out a zoning committee to check her sister's permits—that Jacuzzi was not on any record she remembered seeing. No one could prove that Marvella's business was shady, but as a councilwoman, Delilah felt it was of the utmost importance to see that Lonely Hearts Station retained its promising reputation as a safe, wonderful haven for tourists with a yen for small-town appeal. "Sister, dearest, it's time you and I had a little heart-to-heart, so to speak."

KATY POKED HER HEAD in the kitchen, watching Jerry frost cookies for a minute. "Good morning," she finally said. "Would you like help?"

"No. Yes," Jerry said suddenly. "Take a dozen of these out to Laredo's truck, if you don't mind."

"Why?" She didn't mind, but why were cookies being sent out to Laredo's truck? Was he leaving?

"I'm sure he'll need breakfast eventually. Plus, you can make certain he's still breathing."

"Did he sleep out there all night?"

"And his brothers. I thought they might tie one on, but it was actually pretty quiet." He handed her a plate of cookies.

She looked at the plate in her hands. With a pretty blue napkin on the plate, it looked like a peace offering. That might be a good thing. "Thanks, Jerry."

"No problem." He went back to frosting, his face innocent of intention. After she and Laredo had argued, sugar frosting was likely a good idea.

"Here. Take these bottles of water, too. They can't drink beer with their cookies. Well, they could, knowing them," Jerry said, "but we want to get a reputation for wonderful hospitality. Miss Delilah's thinking about leasing out the spot next door and opening up a bed and breakfast."

"Is she really?" That seemed like a wonderful plan.

"Yeah, but don't let the cat out of the bag. We wouldn't want Marvella messing her up in any way. Delilah got the idea because she's been putting up so many guests lately." He grinned at Katy. "People can't sleep in their trucks forever. And we're having all this interest in the rodeo. I do believe some ideas are blossoming in Delilah's brain.''

"I'll be certain not to say a word.'' She went outside to Laredo's truck. Two cowboys were in the truck bed, snoozing like dogs on a lawn. One cowboy, the one she was interested in, was facedown in the back seat, with all the windows ventilating him.

"Laredo,'' she said through the window. "Laredo! Are you all right?''

"I'm fine,'' he said without looking up. "Go away.''

"I've got frosted cookies.''

He sat up. "Don't go away.''

She handed him the plate. "You're supposed to share with your brothers.''

He bit into a cookie and hid the plate on the floorboard. "In my home, we learned quickly that it was every man for himself. By the way, I've been thinking about our standoff.''

"Our standoff?''

"Yeah.'' He licked his fingers. "Me rematching and you posing. It's not a fair threat, because I really want to do this and you really don't want to get naked. What would your parents say? And your ex-fiancé?''

She felt her face go pale at the thought of Stanley staring at her nude body. Just that image alone caused every reasonable argument she could conduct with herself to disappear. Ugh. Never, never, never.

But Laredo didn't have to know he'd just called

her bluff. "We can talk about this another time," she said icily. "Please don't try to prey on my mind, either. It's beneath you."

"Not really." He snagged another cookie and stared at her newly shortened dress. "I like you in blue."

"Thanks. I like you when your eyes aren't red from sleeping in your truck."

"I didn't sleep well. Ranger bangs around like a bad drum in his sleep, and his boots kept crashing against the truck bed. I think Tex snores louder than Jerry."

She examined her nails. "Are you complaining or hinting?"

"Both."

She shrugged at him. "My bed is still available." And her body, but Mr. Big Thing had to make the first move.

"I may take you up on it. By the way, I've had a new idea."

Her brows went up.

"I'm going to call that nice doctor back, the one who treated me in the hospital, and I'm going to ask her to the rodeo this weekend."

Katy's blood pressure was going to need treatment if Laredo was going where she thought he was. "In case you hit your head again, you'll have your own personal medical team on standby?" she guessed.

"Nah. I'm going to invite her to bring the hospitalized kids out, the ones who are long-term but mobile enough to attend, to see the rodeo. They'd probably get a kick out of that."

Katy's mouth dropped open. "Laredo—"

"It's a charity event, after all. We should include the ones who would enjoy it the most."

She didn't know what to say.

"The tickets can be on me."

"I'm sure Delilah could wring one of her new sponsors for the tickets," Katy murmured. "What made you think of this idea?"

"My ever-present headache. I was feeling sorry for myself, and then I remembered those kids in the hospital, and I realized rodeo is for kids. I'm just a big kid, you know."

"I had figured as much," she murmured, touched by his idea.

"I want to be more than just a one-time thing," he said earnestly. "I want to be a gladiator. I want to matter. I want to do something with myself, something—"

"I know, I know," she said, "something big." Sighing, she gazed into his face. "Laredo, it's a wonderful idea. You need to mention it to Delilah and see what she thinks, but I believe she'll be delighted. And I'll bet Jerry would love to offer his driving services for the kids."

He perked up. "I hadn't thought of that. You know, me and you, we're an okay team."

She backed away from the truck. "I don't think so, actually. Just because a few of our ideas mesh doesn't make us interlocking pieces."

"Well, we haven't gotten to that yet—"

"And we probably won't," she said, turning to race back inside. Her heart beating hard, she ran up to her room and closed the door behind her. "Oh, Rose," she said to the mouse she'd rescued from Bloodthirsty's hooves, "I think I just lost my heart for good."

"LAREDO'S MIND revolves around doing something big," Katy told Hannah an hour later as they sat in Katy's room.

"And your mind revolves around him."

"Precisely. I feel like I'm trying to stop him from being on a path to himself."

Hannah shrugged. "All you want to do is hug him and kiss him and squeeze him a little. What's wrong with that?"

Katy stared at her friend. "You make him sound like a teddy bear, which he most certainly is not."

"So quit being such a chicken. He can take a break from being Sir Galahad long enough to rescue you from—what did you call it? The phallic tower you live in? And don't forget, you have a goal, too. To be the greatest chemistry professor Duke has ever seen."

She frowned. "I'm going from one tower to another."

"Yeah, but college can't really be considered a phallic symbol," Hannah pointed out. "I mean, can it?"

"What I mean is that I'm going from one clois- tered, safe existence to another."

"I don't know that academics can be considered safe. At some universities it may be more of a po- litical lion's den. Are you sure you know what you're getting yourself into?"

Katy closed her eyes. "Safety. Stay the course."

"That's right," Hannah soothed. "The well-proven path."

Katy opened her eyes when a knock sounded at the door. "Come in," she called.

Laredo walked in, and her breath tightened in her chest.

"Well, I must be going," Hannah said, quickly getting up and exiting. "Bye, Laredo."

"Bye," he said as she left. "Katy, can we talk?"

"Sure."

He closed the door behind him, which suddenly made her nervous, although she couldn't say why. Laredo hadn't made the remotest attempt to seduce her or even kiss her in days. Not since the day at the creek, in fact. And even that wasn't a serious attempt, or it would have happened.

"Katy, I've been thinking about this *Playboy* problem."

"Oh?" Not a good time to tell him it was no longer a problem, she supposed. Better to hear him out. Was it possible he was actually jealous of the thought of her being naked for other men?

"Have you called the photographer back yet?"

"Uh, no."

"Okay. Well, when will you?"

She shrugged, her mind moving quickly. "Tomorrow?" she asked. "Does that sound like a good time? It'll be Monday, after all."

He nodded. "Perfect. Okay. Bye."

And then he left.

She stared at the door he'd closed behind him. He'd sounded strangely as if he didn't care anymore, as if he'd been gathering remote information for a file. Of course, he was basically saying, "I'm riding, so you're posing. That's the gauntlet you threw down, so go ahead and do your deal."

And she had too much pride to tell him just thinking of Stanley had illustrated how stupid her idea to get wild in that manner had been.

It was enough to make her cry. She'd never been so confused in her life. Part of her was positive she had no business falling in love since she'd just been burned, but the problem was, since Laredo, she'd realized she wasn't on the rebound.

She'd never loved Stanley. And Laredo had stolen her heart.

Yet he didn't seem to want it.

"I NEED Y'ALL to do me a favor," Laredo told his brothers when he went back out to the truck.

"Now what?" Tex demanded crustily.

"I need you to sleep in Katy's bed tomorrow night. One of you, at least."

Both of his brothers instantly raised their hands.

Laredo grimaced. ''Not like that. I need you to be in her bed as a decoy.''

''Where will she be?'' Tex asked with interest.

''I'm taking her to Malfunction Junction. She'll be safe there,'' Laredo replied.

''Is she in danger?'' Ranger sat straight.

''Only from herself. But I'll be there to protect her,'' Laredo said with satisfaction.

''Oh, yeah, that's great protection. She'll be glad to hear it, I'm sure,'' Tex said with a smirk.

''Actually, Katy isn't going to hear it.'' This was a detail Laredo had hoped to leave out, but it didn't seem as if that would be possible.

His brothers raised their brows and waited in silence.

Laredo sighed. ''She's planning on posing for *Playboy Magazine.*''

Their jaws dropped in tandem.

''What month?'' Tex demanded.

Not for the first time, Laredo thought about doing damage to his twin. ''She's not going to pose for *Playboy*. This is not the way she is going to become wild and crazy, which is her mission in life at this time.''

Ranger whistled. ''You're going to stop her?''

''Right. But I have to be careful about how I do this, because she's trying to stop me from my mission in life, which is to do a Big Thing, which is to stay on Bloodthirsty Black until the horn. So that I can save Miss Delilah's salon,'' he finished with a verbal flourish.

"Oh, yeah, the one-man cavalry. We forgot about that." Tex smirked. "Okay. Let us get this straight. You're going to girlnap Katy from under Miss Delilah's very wary nose and lock her into a tower at Malfunction Junction while you ride that bull until your heart's content."

"Right." Laredo nodded, happy that his family was so quick on the uptake.

"You are being a typical male, and I think it would serve you well to think over your plan for ruts," Ranger informed him. "I don't think Miss Katy's going to cotton to it."

"Are you recommending I should let her pose?" Laredo was outraged. If so, these were not the brothers he cared to claim.

"I'm stating that you can't have your cake and eat it, too," Ranger said mildly. "You can't do your thing and expect her not to do hers."

"Mine doesn't involve shedding clothing! Mine doesn't involve people gawking over my naked physique!"

Tex laughed. "That's presuming anyone would gawk."

"Well, they'll gawk at Katy, and I don't like it," Laredo stated stiffly. "You just figure out another way I can handle this matter, then, wisenheimers."

"No, no." Ranger held up a hand. "We don't interfere, we only participate when needed. It's your life, it's your funeral, 'cause she is surely going to kill you as you try to drag her off. But hey, we've always been a family for the rowdy choice, so I vote you go for it. I'll sleep in Katy's bed and do a convincing Katy voice when Miss Delilah does bed check.''

"She doesn't actually do bed check," Laredo said stiffly, ''but Rose the mouse will need to be fed and watered.''

The brothers stared at him. "Oh, no," Ranger said. "I didn't agree to mother hen a mouse.''

"Oh, hell," Tex said. "I'll baby-sit the damn mouse and play Katy in the night."

Laredo frowned at his brother. "I didn't particularly like the phrasing of your statement.''

"I'm going to sit in my truck and laugh my butt off as you drag Katy kicking and screaming out of here," Ranger said. "Remember, the doctor said you were to suffer no further damage to your head, and that includes female inflicted. So when does this plan go down?''

"Friday night," Laredo said grimly. "I can keep her busy until then. After that, I'll be busy at the rodeo and I won't be able to keep a direct eye on her. Plus, she told me that if I rematched, she'd pose. So I have to get her out of here before I ride Saturday. Helga can keep an eye on her.''

Because she was just prissy enough to take a train out of there Saturday afternoon after he hit the dirt. That was one lady who couldn't be trusted to let a man get away with living his life the way he chose.

He wasn't about to let her get away that easily.

Certainly not to display her charms to every Tom,

Dick and Harry on the planet. He felt ill just thinking about that!

No way. If there was going to be a first in her life, she needed a winner. Not another loser like ol' Stanley.

That was the hero in him talking—the rescuer. The real underlying reason, as he would barely allow himself to acknowledge, was that he saw red when he considered the possibility of another man touching her, even on paper.

He wanted her all to himself. Not forever. Just long enough for him to figure out why he couldn't stop thinking about her. And wanting her enough to make him dizzy and desperate at times.

Dizzy. Desperate.

But not, he told himself, forever.

He'd seen what passed for forever, and he knew too well that there was no such thing. Like Santa Claus and fairy tales, he couldn't waste emotion believing in them.

It was all about trust. And he knew trust and forever didn't go together. Katy knew it, too, thanks to Stanley. She was looking for a second forever, though, like a sweet little lamb being led to slaughter. Oh, she denied it, but it was there in the hope in her eyes. Exactly what the *Playboy* photographer had seen. Vulnerability.

Laredo shook his head to clear the buzzing. If he didn't get Katy to himself real soon, he was certain he was going to go mad.

Chapter Fifteen

"Heart-to-heart?" Marvella asked.

Delilah nodded. The two of them hadn't spoken a direct word to each other in maybe fifteen years. Her sister had changed, her face leaner and perhaps more withdrawn than Delilah remembered. But she had been close to her older sister as a child, which made their emotional separation and Marvella's destruction all that much more heartrending.

"Go for it," Marvella said. "But make your heart-to-heart quick. My schedule is full. We've picked up forty percent from the rodeos."

"Which brings me straight to the point. Your schedule is full because of my cowboys."

"Your cowboys?" Marvella smiled and sat down, not offering Delilah a seat. "How do you figure? Your bull hasn't won in two separate weeks. I'd say it's Bad-Ass Blue that's garnering the attention. He's well on his way to being a superstar, I'd say."

Marvella examined her long, pretty nails. Even at her age, she was an attractive woman. If only her eyes held more love for mankind, she could even be called gracefully aged.

"All the better for his sale price. I love profit, don't you?" Marvella asked coyly.

Delilah shook her head. Maybe a few die-hard rodeo buffs were coming to see the winning bull, but the real magic lay in the charming town. The Jefferson brothers had added fairy dust. Of course, Marvella's salon would be pulling more extra business—Tex had ridden the winning bull.

"Marvella, I want this weekend's rodeo to be fair. No cheating, no dirty tricks. My cowboy has a concussion, and he shouldn't be riding at all. I think it would behoove us to let the best man win without interference."

Marvella shrugged. "I have no idea what you're talking about. Tex offered to ride Blue on his own."

Sure. After Cissy had softened him up. Delilah sighed. "Look. This is between you and me. It has nothing to do with our employees, the Jefferson brothers or Lonely Hearts Station. We should settle our differences like ladies."

Marvella's gray eyes suddenly glowed with heat. "How dare you suggest that I am not a lady? Who slept with whose husband, Delilah dear?"

Delilah didn't answer. It was true that Marvella's husband had divorced Marvella to marry her. But the circumstances were not as Marvella cared to paint them. The trouble was Marvella seemed quite content to blame Delilah for the downfall of her marriage.

"Would you say that your behavior was becoming of a lady?" Marvella asked smoothly. "I mean, I wouldn't. I would classify you more as a... husband-stealing hussy."

Outrage bubbled inside Delilah. She forced herself to remain calm. "Name-calling isn't going to get us anywhere. I'm worried about Tex and Laredo and—"

"They're big boys," Marvella snapped. "Quit trying to mother everybody on the planet. It's annoying, it's manipulative and it bores me."

Delilah blinked. "Can I assume that you intend to remain busy with your bag of tricks?"

Marvella stared at her. "I have no idea what you're babbling about, but it sounds like poor sportswomanship to me."

The sisters held each other's gaze for several seconds. "You know," Delilah said suddenly, "I'm not certain that Jacuzzi or some of the other accoutrements of this room have a permit. Do you happen to know if your permits are up-to-date, Marvella? And could you swear in a court of law that your business is reputable?"

Marvella smiled thinly at her. "Delilah, don't try to use your seat on the council to threaten me. All the town fathers have been to my salon, my dear. They're not all regulars, but..." She let her words trail off.

Delilah stared at her sister, a sinking feeling inside.

"We do give good service," Marvella finished

with a laugh. "And it's *all* about service. You know, I think that's the real reason you're here. You're going under, and you want a shoulder to cry on. Unfortunately, I can't stand poor sportswomanship in business, either. Did you care for my feelings when you stole my husband, sister?"

The look in Marvella's eyes was so determined and so cold. Involuntarily, Delilah felt a shiver go through her. She really had no defense against this much hatred. There was no recognition of warmth, of childhood memories. Marvella was locked in her own world of revenge.

"I'm sorry I came," Delilah said, completely regretting seeing how her sister had changed.

"Well, I'll see you on Saturday, Delilah, dear," Marvella said. "See you *lose.*"

"I DON'T TRUST HIM," Katy said, busily picking the lock on the storage area in Laredo's truck bed. "He's planning to ride, and it doesn't matter what the doctor says, he's bound and determined to give himself the permanent stupids."

"Why do you care?" Hannah asked, squinting at Katy's handiwork and surreptitiously watching the street should any Jefferson brother happen to amble by.

"I care for two reasons. First of all, I got him into this. He's only doing it out of a sense of duty."

"I don't know. He seemed genuinely determined to ride Bloodthirsty again."

"Well, he's got hero syndrome. Bad, too, I might add."

"Are you going to cure him of it?"

"Nope." The storage bin popped open, and Katy gasped.

"What's in there?"

She'd been expecting to see his gear, which she planned to filch so he couldn't possibly ride. What she found instead was nothing. "It's empty."

"And his stuff isn't in your room."

Katy shook her head. "He's been sleeping in his truck with his brothers. Sometimes they drive off and don't come back until the morning. I thought maybe they've been going back to Union Junction at night, but I haven't gotten up the nerve to ask."

"Well, he has to have equipment."

"Yes." Katy closed the trunk and relocked the lock. "He's one step ahead of me somehow."

Hannah climbed up into the trunk bed. "Okay, his vehicle is here. He is not. But he could be someplace trying on his gear. He could be training to ride Bloodthirsty."

"Do you think he'd take that chance? He knows his brains are already scrambled."

Hannah shrugged. "I don't think we fully comprehend the minds of men. Don't waste your time. So, what was your second reason for doing this, before your plan went belly-up?"

"That I've fallen in love with him," Katy said slowly. "Stupidly, impossibly, in love with him.

Which is really the dumbest thing I've ever done, up to and including trying to marry Stanley.''

"Oh, boy,'' Hannah said. "You were just supposed to have him rid you of your virginity. You were supposed to remember that he has a wandering foot. You weren't supposed to stray from the course.''

"I know. What makes it worse is that he doesn't care about me at all. He didn't even care about me posing for *Playboy*.''

"So, are you going to?''

"No. I thought about Stanley looking at my naked body, and I felt genuinely ill. I'm not nude model material.''

"You could tell him,'' Hannah suggested.

"Tell him what?''

"That you're in love with him.''

Katy blinked. "And he would die of embarrassment. This is a man who is riding a bull out of an overinflated sense of duty. What do you think he does for a woman who burdens him with her emotions?''

"Says, 'Me, too'?''

She shook her head. "No. He hits the road in his shiny truck and he never even glances in his rearview mirror.''

"Oh.'' Hannah sighed. "Well, if you can't steal his gear, and you can't tell him the truth, then what have you got?''

"Nothing,'' Katy said miserably. "It's all about

trust, and I forgot how to trust anyone. Then when I found somebody worth trusting, I blew it.''

"You don't know that you've blown it yet," Hannah soothed.

"It feels blown like an old tire."

"Well, here he comes, so puff yourself back up."

Katy straightened, not able to help herself from looking too eager. "He's wearing his gear, the snake!" she whispered to Hannah.

"I know how you can steal it!" Hannah whispered back.

"How?"

"Play strip poker. You can borrow my cards."

Katy blinked as Laredo and his brothers neared. It was like looking at a mirage of the best-looking, toughest cowboys one could imagine simply appearing like magic in the middle of the dusty town street. Her mouth watered. "No strip poker. It's too risky. He'd probably win."

"Then just strip him, Katy. Like I stripped y'all the night we went to the creek. Be brave!"

"Be brave?" She had a mouse for a pet. She wasn't the type of girl to roar and break things and raise hell.

"Hey, ladies," Laredo said as they reached the truck. All the brothers tipped their hats, but Laredo's smile seemed to turn to a grim, determined line as he looked at Katy. "What are you doing in my truck? Stealing my beer?"

"Exactly," Katy said, trying to match his teasing tone. And yet, his eyes were not smiling for her.

"So, where have you handsome cowboys been?"

"We rode some horses over to the hospital and did some lasso tricks for the kids," Ranger said. "Laredo wanted to talk to the doctor who treated him."

Something burning seemed to lodge in Katy's heart, although she told herself it was silly to be jealous of the beautiful physician. "Did you tell her you were going to ride in a couple of days?"

"Yes, ma'am." He tipped his hat and looked at her. "And she said I was a fool, but that there was no prescription for that, so she would come to watch in case I needed a physician on hand."

"His own personal physician." Tex laughed. "None of us have ever had one of those."

"None of you have ever needed one, maybe," Hannah snapped. "Laredo's already hurt."

Katy couldn't take her eyes off Laredo. "She's coming to watch you?" That seemed medically sacrilegious on the doctor's part, which meant the jealousy spiking hot inside Katy's head would probably measure as a fever on a thermometer.

"Yep, and she's bringing a bunch of kids. Actually, she's organizing it, and Jerry's going to help out."

He looked so pleased with himself that Katy felt ashamed.

"So," he said, "called *Playboy* yet?"

Her mouth dropped open at the surprising change of subject. "No, actually I haven't."

He walked away, whistling. "Let me know what

you find out when you do," he called over his shoulder.

"Guess we're heading to the cafeteria," Ranger said. "See you soon." He and Tex headed off after Laredo.

Hannah's eyes narrowed as she stared after Laredo. "That man is way too casual."

"What do you mean?"

"I don't know. I don't trust him."

Katy got down from the truck, her feelings totally blasted. "He doesn't care about me anymore, Hannah. Maybe he never did. Certainly after he took that whack on the head, things have changed. Either it's the doctor he met, or he knocked himself hard enough to forget that he ever wanted to make me a bikini top from beer caps. Or he wasn't that interested to start with. But I'm not going to moon around after a man who doesn't want me."

She headed toward the salon. Hannah hurried up beside her. "So, what are you going to do? Call *Playboy*?"

Katy winced. She wished she'd never thought that she could unleash her inhibitions in such a manner. The truth was, she was exactly what Stanley had said she was: less tempting than a day-old biscuit.

Frigid.

"I'm leaving," Katy announced. "It's time I took a leaf out of Laredo's book and headed out to do my own Big Thing. But you can't tell a soul."

LAREDO AND HIS BROTHERS crouched in the doorway of a nearby feed store, watching Katy and Hannah go inside the salon. "They're up to something," Laredo said. "What do you think they were really doing in my truck?"

"I don't know," Ranger said thoughtfully. "Hannah had so much mischievousness gleaming in her eyes, she looked like a raccoon."

"It's the hair," Tex said. "She's really cute."

"Raccoons are not cute," Laredo said.

"That one is," Ranger agreed. "Although she's a bit too tricky for my taste."

"Tricky?" If anybody was tricky, it was Katy. "At least she doesn't dream of taking off her clothes for major publications," Laredo stated.

"Well, hello, gentlemen," Marvella said as she left the feed store. "How are the famous Jefferson cowboys doing?"

Tex grinned at her, taking the package she was carrying. "We're fine."

"I've been waiting for you to tell me you're riding for me this weekend, Tex," Marvella said. "A repeat would be a wonderful attraction."

"You haven't hired anyone?" Tex asked eagerly. Then his face fell. "Actually, Miss Marvella, I'm afraid I can only ride against my brother once."

"Oh, dear," Marvella said. "I am so disappointed."

"Ride against me once?" Laredo sputtered. "You damn sure better be riding Blue this weekend! I have to beat you. Otherwise, I haven't achieved my goal." Or shown Katy that he could do it.

The brothers followed Marvella over to her salon. "Well, why don't you three come in and we'll talk it over?" she invited. "I think there's some fresh-baked banana bread and mint juleps just waiting for someone to enjoy them."

"I will," Ranger said.

"I sure can," Tex said.

With an uneasy glance toward the Lonely Hearts Salon, Laredo hesitated. But why be rude? This was the other half of the rodeo, which he was doing for Delilah, for Katy, for the sick kids, for Lonely Hearts Station and for himself. "I guess so," he said.

"Excellent," Marvella cooed. "Simply excellent."

Chapter Sixteen

When Marvella walked in towing the three Jefferson cowboys, Cissy knew there was trouble in Texas. Marvella was up to her tricks, and someone was going to get hurt.

There was always an injury in Marvella's shenanigans. Cissy was afraid that if Marvella kept up with her attack, the injury this time was going to be Katy.

Why should she care? she thought. Katy had never been especially warm to her. Not that she'd ever given Katy a chance—and she did try to steal her cowboy.

Maybe that's why she cared. She hadn't felt right about what she'd tried to do to Katy. For some reason, once she'd made love with Tex, her heart had changed. If anything, she wanted to look good in his eyes. Oh, he'd never see her as anything more than a soiled dove, but...even soiled doves craved respect.

Without saying a word to anyone, Cissy slipped outside.

THE KNOCK ON KATY'S DOOR stopped her packing. It didn't sound like Delilah's tap or Hannah's bang. Certainly it wasn't Laredo's unannounced entrance. She supposed that since they technically were splitting a room, he didn't feel he had to announce himself. Then again, that's just how Laredo was. Unannounced.

But one never knew, and she didn't want her plans brought to light. Quickly she pushed the suitcase under the bed. "Come in," she called.

Cissy Kisserton walked in. "Hi, Katy."

"Cissy?" Katy couldn't dampen the surprise in her voice. "What are you doing here?"

"I need to warn you about something."

"Whatever it is, I don't want to know." Uncomfortably she wondered if good manners demanded she offer Cissy a chair. No, she decided.

"You'll want to know this," Cissy assured her.

"Does it have anything to do with Lonely Hearts Station, cowboys or the rodeo?"

"It has to do with Laredo."

Spears of pain shot through her. "I definitely do not want to know about him."

"You don't?" Cissy's tone crept high with dismay. "Why not?"

"Because. It doesn't matter." It did, in a peculiar way she couldn't explain, but she couldn't let him matter to her.

"Oh. I beg your pardon. I shouldn't have bothered you, then."

Katy warily watched her prepare to leave. What

exactly had been the purpose behind Cissy's visit? "He's...all right, isn't he?"

"Oh, yes. Healthwise, he seems very fit."

That was all the assessment she wanted from Cissy, thank you very little. "Then that's all I need to know."

Hannah walked into the room, her mouth gaping when she saw Cissy. "What do you want?"

"Relax, Hannah. This is just a civil conversation between Katy and me."

Hannah glowered at her. "Well, I'm here now. It's no longer civil. What are you up to?"

Katy held up her hand. "Hannah, it's all right. Cissy was just leaving. She came to tell me Laredo is all right."

Hannah raised a brow. "We know he's all right. Since when did you become the Good News Fairy?"

"Since Marvella just dragged him and his brothers into her salon," Cissy said. "But since y'all don't want to know—"

"Wait a minute," Katy said, grabbing hold of Cissy's sleeve. "Spit it all out, every bit of it, or Hannah holds you, and I take a hot curling iron to your hair. You'll look like the dippity-do-dog when I get through with you if you don't stop playing Miss Who-Me?"

"There's no need to get violent!" Cissy said, snatching her sleeve away.

"And you could be the Trojan horse. Spare us the melodramatics and get on with Marvella's hijinks," Hannah instructed. "I saw a curling iron downstairs that's been left on for three days and looks hot enough to brand cattle.''

"I don't know what her plan is! I just know Delilah was there earlier, and the two of them had words. Exactly what words, I don't know, because when Marvella has a guest, we are not allowed to see or be seen. We all went upstairs and left the two of them alone. But the tone of it wasn't friendly, as anyone who knows Marvella would understand. And then Marvella walked in with Tex, Laredo and Ranger, and I thought Katy should know.''

"Why Katy?" Hannah demanded.

"Because I owe her one," Cissy snapped. "Okay? Virtuous enough reason for you?"

"Guilt," Katy pronounced.

"Precisely," Hannah agreed. "Unless someone else is sucking up to Laredo right now and you want even.''

Katy's heart skidded inside her. Could that be the case?

"No one's sucking up to anyone right now. Marvella's plying them with mint juleps and snacks.''

"Then maybe she's just turned over a new leaf, like you," Hannah guessed. "After all, Tex did ride for her. He did make her a lot of money.''

Cissy flipped her long, straight hair. "I've said too much. I'm leaving before I get seen in this salon. What you do with this info is up to you. And for whatever it's worth, while I do hope we win again on Saturday, I never wanted anyone to get hurt.''

She left, her high heels clipping down the stairs.

Hannah turned to Katy. "What do you make of that?"

"I don't know. She expects us to do a search-and-rescue on the Jefferson brothers," Katy said. "But I don't think I could."

"Nor me," Hannah said carefully. "I don't think men appreciate being dug out of their caves, do they? Isn't it kind of like roaches? They skitter away from the light and don't want to be disturbed?"

"Hannah," Katy said, laughing. "This is serious. Marvella is planning to shanghai all the cowboys this time, just to spite Delilah. That'll leave me to do the riding, and I'm not physically up to it. Nor emotionally, I might add. I like having my feet on the ground, not over my head."

"We *could* go save them from themselves," Hannah said thoughtfully. "But you'd think grown men would have more class. More panache. More common sense."

"Why would anyone think that?" Katy asked. "You just compared them to roaches."

"I was only trying to get inside their minds, and the only species I could think of that liked the dark and liked multiplying and liked not being disturbed was roaches." Hannah shrugged. "The point is, you'd think they'd know better."

"We could just let them suffer the consequences of their stupidity," Katy suggested. "It's not our fault if they louse up their chances of riding and winning."

But the cowboys didn't know Marvella like

everyone else did. And like all men, they were suffering under some delusion that she was probably okay underneath all that faux charm.

What they didn't know was that the faux charm covered a layer of war paint so hard it was like a layer of steel sheeting.

"I don't know," Katy said with a sigh. "I can't always be rescuing Laredo. I've got to think of myself now. Back to packing." She retrieved her suitcase from underneath the bed.

"And I can't save the other two. In pairs, they're almost drawn to misadventure."

"So, that's that." Katy tossed some more things into the suitcase. "I'm going to do a little more packing, and then I'm going to sleep. It sounds as if I'll have my bed to myself tonight, and I intend to enjoy it for the last night it will be mine."

"I'm going to miss you, Katy," Hannah said softly. "I can't believe you're going to leave so soon."

"I'll miss you, too, but the truth is, I'm really looking forward to moving on with my life." Katy snapped the suitcase closed, putting it at the foot of her bed. She arranged her traveling clothes on top. "I'm ready for my own adventure."

SOMEWHERE IN THE NIGHT, Tex awakened aware of two things. He was alone, which was a relief, because he felt very stifled somehow. Two, the mint juleps he'd drunk weren't like lemonade, as he'd surmised, judging by the fact that his head felt two sizes bigger than normal.

Where were his brothers? Feeling around, he switched on a bedside lamp. And then he remembered! He was supposed to occupy Katy's bed tonight while Laredo girlnapped Katy! Holy smokes! He'd probably overslept the whole plan. No wonder he was here alone.

Sneaking out of the room, he quietly went down the stairs. Gently he worked the front door of the salon open, praying no one would awaken. How could he have ended up in such shape when Laredo needed him? Most times in the Jefferson household, it was every man for himself, but when it came to brotherhood, they stuck together like soles to boots. He didn't agree with Laredo's plan, necessarily, but he was going to help execute it and let the chips fall where they might.

Laredo's truck was gone from its parking place. Dang! He must have already left with Katy. Tex needed to get a serious move on. He didn't even know what the heck time it was, but he had a mouse to baby-sit and a voice to mimic.

Ever so silently, he took the key Delilah had given him and Ranger and unlocked the Lonely Hearts back door. He crept up the stairs with his boots in his hand, making certain not to make any noise, not even a groan, which he felt like doing. Damn mint juleps! Never again was he falling for some innocent-looking southern libation.

Slowly and silently, he opened Katy's bedroom

door. With cautious feet, he moved to the end of the bed, noting its outline by the light of the streetlamp shining through the window. So far so good. Now, to fall into her bed and sleep until Saturday.

Well, he might get up to swallow some aspirin tomorrow. And then he was hibernating until he knew for certain the coast was clear.

Something at the foot of Katy's bed caught his boot, and to his surprise, he toppled over like a great, drunken redwood tree. He fell right onto something soft—and shrieking.

"Aii—"

"Shh!" he told the shrieking thing, clapping a hand over its mouth. "It's only me!"

"Laredo?" Katy asked.

"What are you doing here?" he demanded.

"Sleeping, you dope! What are you doing here?"

Considering that he was Tex and not Laredo, nothing good. Dang! He was in big trouble now. Did he exit gracelessly? Or did he wait for Laredo to appear and help him bundle Katy off?

No, that would make him a girlnapping accessory, something he didn't want any part of. Bed-sitter was one thing; hands-on accomplice was something else. "It's Tex," he said, choosing the coward's option. "Go easy on me."

Instantly she relaxed. "Oh. Were you looking for Hannah's room?"

Ah! An easy out! "As a matter of fact—"

"Down the hall," she told him. "But I wouldn't fall on her the way you fell on me. She's been known to wallop men who've tried to sneak into her bed before. Try the gentle, romantic approach.''

"I didn't mean to fall on you, Katy. Did I hurt you? I actually tripped over something at the foot of the bed—"

"My suitcase. I shouldn't have left it there. I wasn't expecting visitors—"

"Your suitcase? Why do you have your suitcase out?'' Did she know Laredo was planning on sweeping her off her feet? Wouldn't that just jangle Laredo's nerves if he showed up to snatch Katy and she said, Hold the phone, cowboy, while I get my jammy bag?

"Don't tell anyone, but I'm leaving town," Katy confided.

He knew that already, but maybe it was best if he appeared ignorant. "Oh. Send us a postcard to Malfunction Junction," he said. "We don't often get anything except bills. Well, gotta run."

Trying to appear relaxed and focused, he got out of Katy's bed. He stood up straight, and with as much balance as possible, made his way to the door. "Good night, Katy."

"Good night, Tex."

He left, keeping his pride barely intact. Whew! That was a close one. Only he wasn't certain what he was supposed to do.

Best to leave that in his twin's capable hands. Laredo was the one with the screwy plan, after all.

With a glance at Hannah's door, he told himself not to borrow any more trouble and went into the upstairs den to find the sofa.

Chapter Seventeen

Tex no sooner hit the sofa than he realized there was a bigger problem on his hands, one that the mint-julep haze had disguised. If Katy was in her bed and not girlnapped by his twin, and if his twin's truck was gone, then where the heck was Laredo?

Something had gone awry with the plan, and he wasn't sure how to cope with it. He checked his watch, seeing by the lit dial that it was now actually Friday morning. That, he remembered, was Katy-snatching day.

Getting up, he trudged down the stairs, as quietly as possible. Surely Laredo wasn't too far away. He shouldn't be, if he knew how soft Katy was in her bed. Soft and gentle. Although he hadn't gotten a good sense of her—she was after all his brother's desired, and he had landed on top of her with all the finesse of a sledgehammer—he'd been able to tell enough to know that Laredo was lagging behind when he should be barreling ahead.

"I have to show him everything," Tex muttered.

"The dummy who said that twins are on some emotional wavelength was an idiot."

He went outside just as Laredo's truck pulled up. Ranger and his twin got out.

"Where have you been?" Tex demanded.

"We went for a drive," Ranger said.

"Without telling me?" Tex was totally put out. "Hey, am I in this plan or not?"

"You were at Marvella's. We didn't want to disturb you," Laredo said reasonably.

"Disturb me! I was sleeping off a southern green buzz! Didn't you all feel the kick of those stupid julep things?" Tex demanded.

Ranger and Laredo glanced at each other. "Nah. I didn't drink mine."

"Me, neither," Ranger said. "I'm a beer drinker, though I didn't tell Miss Marvella that."

"Well, I must have taken a little nap." He frowned, thinking about Cissy. Where had she been, anyway? He couldn't remember having seen her but for a split second. In fact, if his memory served, she'd left the salon for a while. "Y'all haven't seen Cissy, have you?"

"Nope. We've been by ourselves since we snuck out," Laredo said. "Are you ready for the big moment?"

"Uh—" Tex tried to sort his scrambled thoughts. "I just came out of Katy's room and she's in there."

"Hey!" Laredo said. "I didn't give you the signal!"

"Sorry. It was the juleps. Anyway, she's already packed and ready to go."

"What are you talking about?" Ranger asked.

Tex shrugged. "Guess she's on to the plan. Or she's leaving Lonely Hearts Station. She definitely said she's leaving. I just thought she meant with you."

"That little minx," Laredo breathed. "She did call that dang photographer! She's leaving to pose!" He sucked in air. "Cover me, brothers. I'm going in."

He took off running toward the salon.

Ranger shook his head. "He's lost his freaking mind. She's going to kill him when he goes busting in her door."

"Yep," Tex agreed, thinking about how disagreeable a female who'd already been awakened and landed on once would be. "She's gonna slap him stupid. So much for avoiding further head trauma."

"Dude," Ranger said, "if I ever fall for a female, please, please, stop me. I do not want to be that insane. That bizarre."

"Hey, it's a deal. We'll commit emotional hara-kiri." They clasped hands, nodding solemnly over their pact, as Laredo came out the door bearing a screeching Katy in his arms.

"Put me down!" she commanded. "Put me down!"

"Go get her suitcase, Tex! She wouldn't let me carry both things at once."

Tex took off at a run, and Ranger started the

truck. "Now, Miss Katy," Ranger said as Laredo put her into the truck, "you be sure and wear your seat belt."

Katy stared at him. "You have all lost your minds. You've been to Marvella's, and you've lost your minds."

"It was the mint juleps," Laredo said. "Never drink anything that sweet. It clogs the brain." He got behind the wheel as Tex tossed her suitcase into the truck bed. "See y'all tomorrow."

He sped away, thoroughly pleased with himself. So far, everything was going according to plan.

"Laredo," Katy said through steely teeth, "if you don't take me back right now, I promise to make your life so utterly miserable you'll think Bloodthirsty Black was a friendly sheep in bull's clothing."

Uh-oh. That didn't sound promising. "Katy, I'm doing what's best for you," he said, trying to sound soothing.

"What's best for me?"

"Yes. Now you just calm down. We'll be to the ranch soon enough."

"You're taking me to your ranch."

He nodded.

"Laredo, you are a dunce."

Wincing, he said, "Well, you and I are fighting, and this is the only way I know to win. It's because you're so darn stubborn, Katy."

"I'm stubborn?" She couldn't believe her ears. On the other hand, she was somewhat flattered that he cared enough to steal her. She had to admit it was much nicer than being jilted. "Why did you tell your brothers you'd see them tomorrow? Are you bringing me back in the morning?"

"Not exactly," he said. "I'm going back."

"You're riding in the rodeo," she said on a gasp. "You stole me so I couldn't leave to pose, but you're riding anyway."

There was no reason to lie. He shrugged.

Rational thought left her. She was trapped. He had played the cards all his way. Just like all the Jefferson men: their way or no way.

It was maddening.

He was watching her for her reaction, and she had one for him—the reaction of a woman who's been pushed to the edge.

She took off her top, and tossed it out the window.

"What are you doing?" Laredo demanded, sounding like something was pinching his throat.

She took off her bra and tossed that out the window, too.

Laredo's jaw dropped, and he slammed on the brakes. "I'll go get it," he said, averting his gaze. "It'll only take me a second. It's such a windy night, we should shut the truck windows."

She laughed at his babbling. "Laredo," she said, "I want you to make love to me. I want you to stop making up excuses. Be brave and make love to me."

"I…I can't."

"Oh, yes, you can," she said. "I always said you'd have to make the first move, but I know you'll never make it. And if you think kidnapping me so you could have your own way was a good idea, I've got a twist for your plan.''

He was staring at her breasts, transfixed. ''Yes, you do. I'm feeling very twisted.''

''You cannot have your cake and eat it, too,'' she told him.

''I don't want any cake right now. I want you to tell me where you want me to make love to you. Name it, anyplace you ever fantasized about, and I'll get you there. Paris, Las Vegas, wherever.''

''The creek,'' she told him. ''I think the creek would be very nice.''

He tried to think if that was appropriate for Katy's first time. Shouldn't there be satin sheets and wine and roses—

''Laredo,'' she said, ''either you start driving or I lose another layer, and as you can see, that would be my shorts.''

''Katy, I'm driving as fast as I can!'' He floored the truck, turning down the road toward the creek. Never had he felt that his truck didn't have enough horsepower, but he couldn't get it to go fast enough. God, she was gorgeous. And she wanted to be his.

It was enough to drive him past sane thought. All his reasons for not making love to Katy flooded out of his mind. He had to stop her now from the foolishness of her plan, and the best way to do that was to keep her very near him.

His plan was foolproof.

He parked the truck at the creek's edge. It was

dark and silent. The trees moved gently in a light breeze. Stars overheard flickered like tiny lights in an inky sea.

"You know, if I was a smart girl, I'd send you down to the creek to check for snakes, steal your truck, go back and collect my top and bra and leave you here," Katy told him. "You deserve it."

He stared at her suspiciously. "Maybe, but…you wouldn't, would you?" Unable to help himself, he drew her to him, touching her lips with a finger, then tracing down to her breasts. "I think I'd blow a fuse if I couldn't have you, Katy Goodnight."

She smiled up at him. "I was hoping you'd feel that way. You've stuck so hard to your plan it was hard to jimmy you loose."

"Well, I'm way loose now."

She opened the truck door. "Come on."

He was out his door in a flash and pulling down the truck gate. Grabbing the blanket from the back, he spread it onto the truck bed floor, then shaped another one into a pillow. Extending his hand, he pulled her up into the bed with him.

"Now, your shirt," she said, gently pulling his off him.

And somehow their lips met, touching, pressing and then pulling. Then all over again, until Katy found herself gasping. "Whew. I didn't know you could kiss like that. Why didn't you do it sooner?"

"I'm questioning that myself right now," Laredo said, gasping as well. "But I'm trying not to think too much about it in case you change your mind."

"My mind! I'm the one who's been trying to get you to do this for weeks!"

"Very unvirginal of you, too, thank heaven," Laredo said, swiftly removing her shorts. "I should have listened to you sooner."

She tugged off his shorts. "You should have listened to me about a lot of things."

"We're not talking anymore," Laredo said, pressing her to the blanket. "There's been way too much of that. All we're doing is feeling. This," he said, rubbing his thumbs over her nipples, "and this," he continued, suckling each of them.

"And this," Katy agreed, running her hand down his chest, down the flat of his stomach, until she reached that part of a man. Taking him in her hands, she treasured the feel of him. "Laredo, I don't really know what I'm doing at this point."

"Argh," he said against her neck, where he'd rested his head when she'd taken hold of him. "What you don't know seems to be a good thing. Don't stop."

She giggled as he kissed down her breasts to her belly. He licked into her belly button, drawing a jerk of surprise from her, then he slipped his tongue inside her, and Katy froze. "Oh, my," she whispered. Any seduction she'd ever planned imploded as he stroked her, building magic feelings she couldn't even put a name to.

When he lifted her higher, giving him greater access to her, strange feelings she'd never felt seemed to freeze her. "Oh, oh," she murmured.

And then she slid over some mysterious brink, hearing herself call Laredo's name like she was afraid to lose him.

Gently he laid her back down, spreading her legs wider and settling himself in between. "Katy," he murmured, "I've dreamed of this for more nights than I can tell you."

He parted her, and slid inside, filling her past the point she thought she could take. She started to cry out, but he covered her mouth with his, taking her breath, taking her pain, and then he began to move inside her, and she mimicked his rhythm, wanting so much to feel his passion. It hurt, but nothing like the emotional things in her life had hurt. To Katy this pain was closeness, and it brought pleasure.

Inside her she felt Laredo growing. A sigh filled her, or least she thought it was a sigh, until the same brink built inside her. Wrapping her legs around Laredo, she buried her face against his shoulder. "Laredo," she murmured. "Laredo!"

"I've got you," he said, holding her tighter, moving deeper inside, penetrating her, driving her into his arms so that she would never want to leave. "Give it to me, baby," he told her. "Relax and let it go."

She trusted him to be there for her. With a surprised cry of rapture, Katy squeezed her eyes shut, feeling the sweet spasms take hold of her.

Her pleasure seemed to excite Laredo all that much more. "Katy," he whispered against her lips. "Oh, sweetheart."

"Laredo, you mean so much to me," she said, kissing him as she felt him beginning to tense. Recognizing that the brink that had claimed her was about to claim Laredo, she held him tighter, squeezing her inner muscles against him.

He moved inside her more fiercely, then suddenly cried out. Katy clung to him as he collapsed against her. Over his shoulder she could see the stars in the heaven, and she knew that all her life she would remember her one night with Laredo.

Chapter Eighteen

Laredo fell asleep on top of her, sleeping like a man well satisfied. Katy smiled tenderly at her cowboy. The fantasy had turned into a wonderful reality.

She wasn't frigid. No way. She'd loved what he'd done to her.

But that was all sex, and she was a liberated woman now. It was time to break out of the rest of her shell.

No man, not even a cowboy like Laredo, was going to one-up her just because he thought he could.

Quietly she slipped his keys from his jeans, which were discarded nearby. She dressed, stealing his top for her own use. Knotting it at her waist, she crawled from the truck bed and got into the truck. When she started the engine, Laredo popped up.

"Hey!"

She locked the doors and floored the truck. Laredo sat down very quickly, realizing he had no choice.

Driving back to town, Katy parked the truck outside the salon. When Laredo jumped down to take possession of his truck, she backed out of the parking space quickly, leaving him standing in the middle of the street, his expression dumbfounded.

Well, maybe it wasn't the best of exits, but she couldn't have allowed him to drag her off to the ranch, anyway. If he wanted to bust his head riding Bloodthirsty, she wasn't going to hang around to watch that, either.

It was time to move on with her life.

"THAT CRAZY GIRL stole my truck!" Laredo complained as Tex and Ranger ran to see why he was standing in the middle of the street with his arms in the air.

"Katy did that?" Ranger asked.

"Yes! Where are your keys? I need to follow her."

Ranger shook his head. "They're upstairs, but you can't use my truck anyway. It's not a good idea to go chasing after a woman with a hot head. You must have made her real mad about something."

"I didn't make her mad. I melted her bones," Laredo said thinly. "She's just so darn stubborn!"

"Where's she going?" Tex asked.

"I have no clue. But that minx stole my truck, and after I made love to her, too!"

That was the biggest insult of all.

Tex and Ranger were staring at him, their mouths open.

"Did you really?" Ranger asked.

"Yes, I did."

"And she drove off without you," Tex said in amazement. "Shew-ee. I hope you ride a bull better than you make love, 'cause clearly you've lost your touch. I never saw a girl run off from you before."

Laredo scratched his head. Hadn't she seemed happy? Satisfied? He shook his head. "She didn't like the kidnapping plan."

"Ohh," they said.

"She made love to you and then she left you holding the sheet," Tex said with some surprise. "That's your favorite trick."

Laredo scowled. "Not exactly true."

His brothers laughed, then walked away.

"Hey, where are you going? You've got to help me find her!"

Ranger waved him off. "You're on your own, Laredo."

This had all come about because of that stupid bull. First, she'd wanted him to ride, then she changed her mind. She wanted a hero, and then she wanted a stud. Who could figure that woman out?

And she'd already told him she wasn't interested in getting serious again, since her blown wedding was only about a couple months cold.

He'd told her he would never be interested in settling down.

It was true. Except then he'd fallen for her scrappiness, and her attitude, and her sweetness. He couldn't completely have her under his thumb. Just when he thought he had her pinned, she pinned him.

"So annoying," he muttered. "A woman should not be driving my truck."

Heaven only knew where she'd taken it. She might never return.

In fact, he knew she wasn't going to. And his heart contracted tightly at the thought. She could have the darn truck if she wanted, although he knew she'd taken it just to make her point. He was overbearing. He was cocky. He had thought he could control the relationship. He might as well have tried to control how hard Bloodthirsty would kick.

KATY WENT TO THE ONE PLACE she knew Laredo wouldn't think to look for her: Union Junction.

More specifically, she headed to her stylist sisters' new salon, Union Junction Style. Beatrice, Daisy, Gretchen, Jessica, Lily, Marnie, Tisha, Velvet and Violet were the brightly painted names above the new hairstyling stations. And every chair was full, both with male and female customers. The salon was buzzing, but almost all talk ceased when she walked in.

"Katy!" they exclaimed. Whichever stylists weren't in the middle of a process rushed over to give her a hug. "What are you doing here?"

"I'm on my way to Duke," Katy said.

"You made up your mind to go," Violet said. She had been unanimously voted this salon's manager.

"Finally," Katy said. "It was past time."

"Can you stay with us for a while?" Marnie

asked. "Before you go become a North Carolinian and we never see you again?"

Katy gulped. "I'd better not," she said. "I've dallied long enough."

Beatrice gave her a hug. "It's that Laredo, isn't it?" she said softly so her Union Junction customers couldn't hear.

"No, I really need to be moving on with my life," Katy protested.

"We heard through the grapevine—" Gretchen said.

"You mean from Hannah," Katy interrupted, knowing Delilah wouldn't gossip.

"The grapevine," Gretchen repeated, "that you and Laredo were engaged in an all-out battle of the sexes. We had our money on you. So what happened?"

Katy was confused. "Money on me? For what?"

"To rope him in," Daisy said. "You know. Marriage."

"Actually, no," Katy murmured. "Marriage was never on either of our minds. It's too soon for me to think of that again, and it will always be too soon for Laredo to think of it. He's got to do his Big Thing, and I needed to find myself. We're sort of on separate tracks that would never permanently connect."

"Oh." Sympathetic murmurs flurried around her.

"Why don't you go in the back and get washed up?" Violet said. "When we're done here, we'll take you to our farmhouse."

"Farmhouse?" Katy asked. "This isn't like Delilah's place?"

"Nope," Tisha said firmly. "It's as different as we could make it. Even down to the name. No more 'Lonely' anything."

"And all the Jefferson boys come to us for their cuts," Velvet said proudly. "We all get one apiece. Except for Last, because he's odd man out, so he rotates amongst us."

"I get him next," Lily said, "and I can't wait!"

"Who cuts Laredo's hair?" Katy murmured, for some reason needing to know silly trivia about the cowboy.

"I do," Violet said kindly. "He's a perfect gentleman, and he's got hair that doesn't want to lie down. Which is fine, because his hat keeps it mashed. And that's all I can tell you about your cowboy, Katy."

Katy flashed grateful eyes at Violet. "Guess I'll go see what you've done in the back."

THE FARMHOUSE was more like a home than Katy would have imagined. "Does Delilah know you've done this? It's wonderful!" she exclaimed.

All the women nodded. "She knows, but she hasn't had a chance to visit. We're pretty proud of it," Velvet said.

"The Jefferson boys helped us find financing, especially Mason," Daisy said. "Mimi actually found us the house. Union Junction has welcomed us with open arms."

"So you're better off here than you were in Lonely Hearts Station." Katy was amazed. "I remember when Delilah had to choose which of us to let go. At the time we thought it was the end of the world."

"We pulled together," Gretchen said, "although don't be fooled. At times we fought like cats and dogs."

They took her upstairs and showed her the bedrooms. "This is such a big farmhouse that we were able to convert extra rooms into bedrooms. Almost all of us have a separate bedroom, and bathrooms are generally shared between only two of us," Beatrice told her. "On the weekends someone usually stops by, either to fix something on the house or bring food."

"They'll never forget us helping them out during the big storm," Katy said. "And it didn't seem like we were doing all that much. Just pulling together."

"Well, we'll always be happy that the e-mail Mimi sent accidentally came to us," Lily said. "Those were some of our darkest days."

Katy sat on a chair in the sitting room, a second-story screened-in porch. She instantly decided it was her favorite room in the house. "I think Delilah has a few more dark days ahead of her, though she would never let on."

"Hannah says that bookings are up," Tisha said.

"A little, yes. But Marvella won the real prize money, and since she's got the winning cowboy, she's getting more of the bookings.'' Katy sighed. ''I thought the good guys always won.''

''So what about Laredo?'' Marnie asked.

Katy stiffened. ''He's riding to the rescue tomorrow.''

''So…what are you doing here?'' Violet asked. ''Don't you want to see him?''

''I don't want to see him get thrown again. I just can't. The doctor was very clear about no more head injuries, but Laredo doesn't listen to anything. He's so stubborn!''

Jessica nodded. ''Stubborn. That's one of your traits, too, you know.''

''Yes, I know, but…what crabs me is that he *could* let Ranger ride. Or someone in his family who knows what they're doing. But no. He's got to be the hero.''

''For you, Katy,'' Jessica said. ''He's trying to be your hero.''

''But I don't want a hero. I want him healthy. I wish I'd never pulled him in off the street. I wish I'd never opened the door and seen him standing out there! I thought I'd seen a miracle, but he turned out to be just a…man,'' she said sadly.

''Why? Because he has no experience? You should give him a second chance,'' Velvet said reasonably. ''Katy, life isn't cleanly cut into right and wrong. Tomorrow he may bust his head open like an egg dropped on cement. Or he could stay on. Who knows? You could admit that you're in love with him. You might risk getting your heart busted open again, or you may end up staying on. He's getting back in the saddle. Why aren't you?''

"Because I'm scared," Katy said. "In the end, I think I'm as big a mouse as Rose.''

"So whose truck are you driving?" Gretchen asked, glancing out the window.

"Laredo's. I stole it from him. But I figure he'll be back here tomorrow night, and then he can pick it up.''

"Uh-huh," Gretchen said. "That's a good idea. Except that he's out front writing on it.''

"Writing on it?" Katy jumped to her feet.

With shoe polish, he'd written all over the truck sides, "Take my truck, but not my heart.''

"Oh, my," Katy murmured. "He is one unstoppable cowboy.''

"Are you going to go down there or not?" Daisy demanded. "That poor man!''

"He's not so innocent," Katy explained. "He was planning on kidnapping me and dumping me at Malfunction Junction so I couldn't leave town and pose for *Playboy.*''

"Good for him," Violet said. "I like that man's way of thinking!''

"You are all against me," Katy said, realization dawning on her as they all waved at Laredo. He stood in the front yard, his hands on his hips, staring up at them.

"No, we're all for finding true love," Lily said.

"I think…I think I'll at least go congratulate him

for outthinking me. And thank him for the use of his truck.''

''You do that,'' Marnie said. ''We'll be waiting up here for you.''

HEART IN HER THROAT, Katy walked downstairs and went out to meet Laredo. ''You found me.''

''I knew where you'd go,'' he boasted.

''Hannah told you.''

''Hannah gave me a couple of bits of insight,'' he admitted. ''She said you probably wouldn't go far from your sisters.''

She stared up at him silently.

''The kidnapping idea was a bad one,'' he said. ''I should have just told you that it killed me to think of your naked body in print. And now that I've made love to you, you leave me no choice. I know you hate to be told anything, but—''

She laid two fingers over his lips. ''I wasn't going to, anyway.''

''Never?'' he asked, moving her fingers, his gaze lighting up.

''Well, I thought about it. I did need to break out of my shell and find out if I was frigid.''

''You're not—''

''But,'' she said quickly, ''once we made love, I knew for sure I couldn't do it. You satisfied that worry in me, and I'll always be grateful for that.''

Laredo grinned. ''I told you.''

She sighed. ''Laredo, you are too confident.''

''I can have confidence for both of us. Until you

get yours back, Katy. You just need someone to stick with you longer than eight seconds.''

"You're still going to ride that darn bull, aren't you?''

"Darn tooting,'' he said. "Me and Bloodthirsty, we've got a date. But I'd like you to be there, Katy.''

She thought about how frightened she'd been when he'd gotten tossed. And then Bloodthirsty had ladled out extra insult by horning him. She thought about how her heart had nearly dried up when he'd been lying on the ground, his expression dazed.

"I'm afraid of that bull,'' she murmured.

"I'm afraid of lots of things.''

"You are not.'' She squinted up at him doubtfully.

"I was damn scared of you being naked for other men, Katy. That's far worse than taking a shot in the pants from a bull.''

She shuddered. It was unbearable to think of it.

"By the way,'' Laredo said conversationally, "I went back and got your bra and top from the side of the road. To be honest, I was afraid when you shucked your clothes like that. I mean, I liked it, but you did kind of goose me, acting all uninhibited like that.''

She didn't believe a word of it. "You didn't act scared.''

"Well, it was kind of a buzz having you throw yourself at me with such determination. Who was I to say no. But I was afraid that you wouldn't like making love to me. That you'd always regret it. You're the kind of girl who thinks too much, Katy. You regretted nearly marrying Stanley, which was very wise of you. But then you regretted pulling me inside the salon and asking me to ride the bull—''

''I only regretted it after you nearly got your head split open,'' she disagreed.

''Irrelevant.'' He held up his hand. ''The point is, then you might have regretted making love with me. This is every man's worst fear, that the woman in his arms will say, 'Gee whiz, I should have stayed home and washed my hair.'''

''Laredo Jefferson!'' Katy stared at him. ''You do not harbor any such doubts. Not behind all that cocky, strutting, everything's-my-way-or-the-high-way attitude. Don't even try to sell me on that!''

''Well, I was reasonably certain I could make you happy,'' he admitted. ''But you still crushed me when you didn't act like you wanted to hang at my bootheels when it was over. You know, follow me around like I was the best thing to happen to you since...you found Lonely Hearts Station.''

She narrowed her eyes.

''Teasing,'' he said quickly. ''Just teasing!''

He had confidence galore to tease her at the moment she most wanted to throw herself at him and beg him not to ride that stupid bull. Beg him to make love to her instead. What a ridiculous situation to have gotten herself into! This man was pigheaded and a little nuts, and here she had fallen for him. Mental note: no more cowboys!

Way too hard on the heart.

"Laredo, if I come watch you tomorrow, will you be happy? Because I really am planning on heading to Duke. And I don't want to keep you from your Big Thing, either. We can be friends, pen pals, even, but I don't want to make love again. Just in case that's what motivated your drive out here."

He shook his head. "That's not why I came here. Had to check on my truck," he said, shining it with the sleeve of his shirt. "No way. It was the last thing on my mind."

Chapter Nineteen

"So, now that we've gotten that out of the way," Laredo said, "can I take you out to dinner?"

He liked the way Katy stared at him. He'd caught her off guard for sure.

"Why?"

Shrugging, he said, "Why not?"

"Because I don't trust you."

"Well, I know that, and good thing you don't, probably." He squinted up at the windows where the new girls in town were staring down at them none too sheepishly. "I could order in chicken for the gang if you want to stay and visit with them."

She nodded. "They'd probably like that."

He smiled at her. "You staying here tonight? There's room at the Malfunction Junction if—"

"No, I think there's plenty of room here," she said. "Thanks just the same."

"You did like it, didn't you?" he asked, just to make certain. His pride was taking a beating, and he was trying to cover the heart on his sleeve, but he was pretty certain he just needed to be patient with Katy. She was like a wild doe that didn't want anyone to get too close.

He could be patient.

"I did," she said softly. "It was wonderful. Thank you for being my first."

No problemo, he thought, because he was darn sure going to be her last. "Fine, fine," he said cheerfully. "Shall I run go get that chicken?"

"If that's what you feel like for your last meal," she replied primly.

"All right, then. Hey," he called up to the girls framed in the screened-in porch.

"Hi, Laredo," they all called back.

"I was thinking about making a run for some fried chicken. Shall we have dinner?"

"Shall we!" Violet called back. "We'll rustle up some margaritas to go with it, if you'd like."

"Nothing better!" He looked at Katy. "Ride with me, pen pal."

She gave him the most suspicious glare he'd ever seen her wear. "Pen pal?"

"Isn't that what you said we could be from now on?"

"Sure," Katy said. "Pals is perfect."

He grinned. The definition didn't matter. He wasn't really a bull rider, and if he and Bloodthirsty worked things out, Katy wasn't really going to be his pen pal, either.

"So, ARE YOU NERVOUS about tomorrow, Laredo?" Violet asked. The weather was perfect for an outdoor picnic, so they all sat on the screened porch, eating fried chicken and drinking margaritas. Katy put down her drink, waiting for Laredo's answer. She certainly was nervous.

"Heck, no," he said. "I think I've got it figured out."

"Is this your last bull ride?" Daisy asked.

He shrugged. "I don't think so. Now I see why Mason always wished we hadn't taken up the sport. I kind of wish I'd taken it up years ago."

Katy stared at him. "Why?"

"I don't know. It's a challenge. Maybe if I had done rodeo, I wouldn't be feeling this urge for a Big Thing now."

Clearly she was not a Big Thing in his life, which was something of a bitter fact for her.

"In fact, I'm going to talk to Miss Delilah about turning Bloodthirsty Black into a bounty bull. I'm pretty sure he might have the makings for it. We'd have to run several more cowboys on him, but if he keeps bucking like he did me, he'll be hard for anyone to ride."

Tight nerves crept inside Katy's stomach. "You know what? It's been a long day for me. I think I'll turn in."

"Come on," Gretchen said quickly. "I'll show you where you're going to sleep."

"Goodbye, Laredo," Katy said. "Good luck tomorrow."

He grinned at her, and her heart did a bellyflop. "Thanks, sweetheart."

All her friends' eyebrows shot up, but Katy paid

no attention. He'd called her that before—and it hadn't meant a thing.

KATY RODE IN with her friends to see Laredo ride. She couldn't remember being this nervous last week. No doubt it had to do with knowing Laredo shouldn't hit his head, the beautiful doctor in attendance or maybe just knowing this was the last time she'd ever see him.

When Tex rode out on Bad-Ass Blue and rounded up another eighty-nine, the arena went crazy. It was triple-packed this weekend due to increased publicity, and the cheers were enthusiastic and loud.

Katy felt ill.

Then she saw Laredo loading into the chute, wrapping his hand. He gave a nod, and Bloodthirsty Black jumped into the arena, snorting fire and kicking flame.

Laredo lasted all of three seconds before he hit the dirt, but this time he landed upright and jumped onto a wall before Bloodthirsty could horn him.

Katy breathed a sigh of relief that felt like it came up through the soles of her feet. The arena cheered and clapped as enthusiastically as they had for Tex. Katy smiled as Laredo waved at the crowd. As he'd said, he liked rodeo, and apparently, it liked him. Even Bloodthirsty had to give up another second to Laredo.

It was a Big Thing to conquer one's fear.

Quietly she sneaked out. Her bag was already packed from the night before. She'd already said goodbye to Delilah and Hannah and the other girls this morning. Jerry was waiting to drive her into town to the airport.

She got on her plane and headed toward her new destination.

A MONTH LATER Katy was starting to settle in. She'd come to North Carolina and fallen in love with the town where the college was located. The staff had been welcoming, the people helpful, the alumni enthusiastic. She'd had an opportunity to take over for a chemistry professor who was on sudden sick leave, and she'd jumped at the chance to ease herself in this way.

It was all going so well, Katy thought. She felt very blessed to have finally found her path. It had taken her a while, but she'd met a lot of wonderful people, and she didn't regret a thing.

Except, perhaps, not seeing the smile on Laredo's face whenever she appeared. He'd made her feel different…and special. She did miss him.

And she missed her friends. And Rose, who was in Delilah's safekeeping.

But it was nice to be getting to know—and like— herself. Already she knew she could be a talented professor.

"Professor Goodnight," a voice said from the back of the lab, "I wonder if you could help me with this test result. It doesn't seem to be coming up the way it should."

She turned and saw Laredo smiling at her.

She should have been surprised, but she wasn't. "What are you doing here, cowboy?"

"Saying hello to a friend."

"You're not a very good pen pal," she told him.

"There wasn't a need. I was on my way here. I left right after the rodeo. My truck and me, we've seen a lot of history, and a lot of sights between there and you."

"Do any Big Things?"

He shook his head. "You?"

She shook her head as well. "Not really."

"Katy," Laredo said, taking her hand, "I'm not chemistry smart. But I do know about emotional chemistry, and you and I have got it in bulk. I think we could have it for the long haul. I'm thinking marriage is a really Big Thing, though, that I'd probably need a partner to help me with. I need you," he said, kissing her fingers.

Tears jumped into her eyes. "I've missed you. But I was mad at you, too."

"I know. I knew it the minute Bloodthirsty tossed me off. I got out of that ring thanking God I still had my head on straight enough to come after you. I knew I was going to do it. I just wanted to make certain you had enough time to follow your dream, the way you let me follow mine."

She took a deep breath that hesitated somewhere in her rib cage. "I thought you wanted to keep riding rodeo. They say all men do."

"Not this man. Ranger's riding next. It's turning out to be quite a cash cow for Lonely Hearts Station, if you'll pardon the pun."

A slow smile lifted her lips. "For my partner, anything."

"Anything?"

"Mmm."

He pulled her into his arms and took a jeweler's box out of his pocket. "Turn this lump of carbon into a diamond, Professor?"

She opened the box, gasping at the two-carat emerald-cut diamond lying inside. "Oh, Laredo," she said, "you're going to make me break down and say it, aren't you?"

He kissed her, taking her face between his hands so he could hold her as close as possible. "Yes."

"I love you," she murmured. "I have since the day I met you."

"I've loved you since the day I saw you mopping up water in Union Junction. I fell in love with your butt."

She smiled as he slipped the ring on her finger. "I fell in love with yours when Bloodthirsty tossed you. You looked so cute going head over heels."

They looked at each other and laughed. And then he picked her up and carried her outside into the North Carolina sunlight.

"We're going to love it here," Laredo said with a smile. "Professor Sweetheart."

* * * * *

Turn the page for a sneak preview of
RANGER'S WILD WOMAN (HAR 986)
the next book
in Tina Leonard's miniseries,
COWBOYS BY THE DOZEN.
Available September 2003.

Prologue

The beautiful old chapel in Union Junction was filled to standing room only. It seemed that every man, woman and child had come to see Sheriff Cannady's sole child wed. Even Delilah and her Lonely Hearts gang had come to fill in as mother and sisters to Mimi. In fact, they'd pretty much taken over the baking, the decorating and, Mason had heard, the choosing of Mimi's trousseau.

According to Last—who'd been as thick into the preparations as Delilah's crew, though that was more the lure of the women than fascination with wedding plans—the wedding night nightie was a heart attack of epic proportions.

Guaranteed to make a grown man go weak at the knees and rock hard in the—

Mason forced his thoughts away from the dangerous wedding night nightie. He shifted uncomfortably in the pew, thinking he'd rather be tied to a stake in the Alaskan wilderness with honey on his toes as lure for wild animals. Anywhere but here in this flower-filled chapel. But because of duty, for the sake of years of friendship and for Mimi, he was here to see her marry another man.

His whole body felt strangely weak, weirdly ill and past the point of medicinal assistance. He was sweating through his black suit, and so nervous his feet were cold-prickling, like straight pins were sticking through his shoes. Truth was, he was lucky as all get-out that he wasn't standing up there in the groom's hot spot. Obviously, Mason was suffering vicarious wedding jitters, no doubt symbiotic empathy for the fear that was surely coursing through Brian O'Flannigan and telepathing to Mason.

How fortunate that he was sitting here in the front row, the position of family favor, while Brian was standing there, about to be yoked.

Mason resisted the uncharacteristic urge to bite his nails. Crack his knuckles. Or even sigh.

His nine unmarried brothers sat beside him in the pew, their postures as rigid and unmoving as his.

Behind him sat Annabelle and Frisco Joe, as well as Laredo and Katy. Helga was baby-sitting Emmie at home.

Ranger had tried to talk to Mason about Mimi, as had Last. In fact every one of his brothers seemed to think he was playing the coward's role, that he needed to do something about Mimi's marriage.

He had no intention of doing a thing. She was doing exactly what she should. Mimi and Mason were best friends, and no third party could ever really change that.

Nor would Mason have changed it. One didn't marry their best friend. No point in ruining a wonderful, since-childhood friendship by asking more of it than it ever could be.

Marriage was messy.

Not to mention he had nine younger unmarried brothers to look after. They might not be children, but sometimes they acted like it, and he needed to keep them as his total focus. Add to that the fact that the family was now beginning to grow, with wives and children, and he had more responsibility than ever.

Matters were fine just the way they were.

And yet, when Mimi floated down the aisle on Sheriff Cannady's arm, passing by Mason with the sweetest, happiest smile on her face—she smiled *right* at him—her expression all glowing, it seemed heated pitchforks speared his heart. Pierced it to pieces.

God, she was lovely. More beautiful than he'd ever realized.

Maybe all his brothers were right. Maybe he did have his head lodged firmly in an unmentionable part of his anatomy. He meditated on this as the ceremony progressed, his ears not hearing any of the words being spoken until the minister's voice rose dramatically, perhaps even pointedly.

"If any person can show just cause that Mimi Cannady should not wed Brian O'Flannigan, speak now or forever hold your peace."

The chapel was deathly silent, so eerily still that

Mason could hear his own heartbeat *thud, thud, thud* in his ears. His suit went from merely hotter-than-hell to a prison of boiling fire as every eye in the church seemed to pin itself to him. Even Reverend Kendall glanced his way, though surely not with any meaning.

Speak now or forever hold your peace.

He tapped his fingers on his knee.

Say it or forever keep a doofus, Uncle Mason smile on your face every time you see Mimi, he thought, which will be often, since she'll be living right next door, like always. He would smile when she became pregnant. And when she proudly watched her children take their first steps. And when she taught them to ride their ponies. And when she had birthday parties for them. And when she grew gray and contented with her husband, forty years from today.

Speak now or forever hold his peace!

Mason cleared his throat.

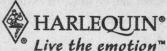

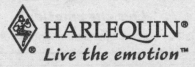

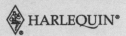

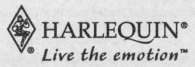

eHARLEQUIN.com

Your favorite authors are just a click away
at www.eHarlequin.com!

- Take our **Sister Author Quiz** and
  we'll match you up with the author
  most like you!

- Choose from over 500
  author **profiles!**

- Chat with your favorite authors
  on our **message boards.**

- Are you an author in the making?
  Get advice from published authors
  in **The Inside Scoop!**

- Get the latest on **author appearances**
  and tours!

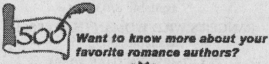

*Want to know more about your
favorite romance authors?*

Choose from over 500 author profiles!

**Learn about your favorite authors
in a fun, interactive setting—
visit www.eHarlequin.com today!**

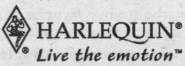